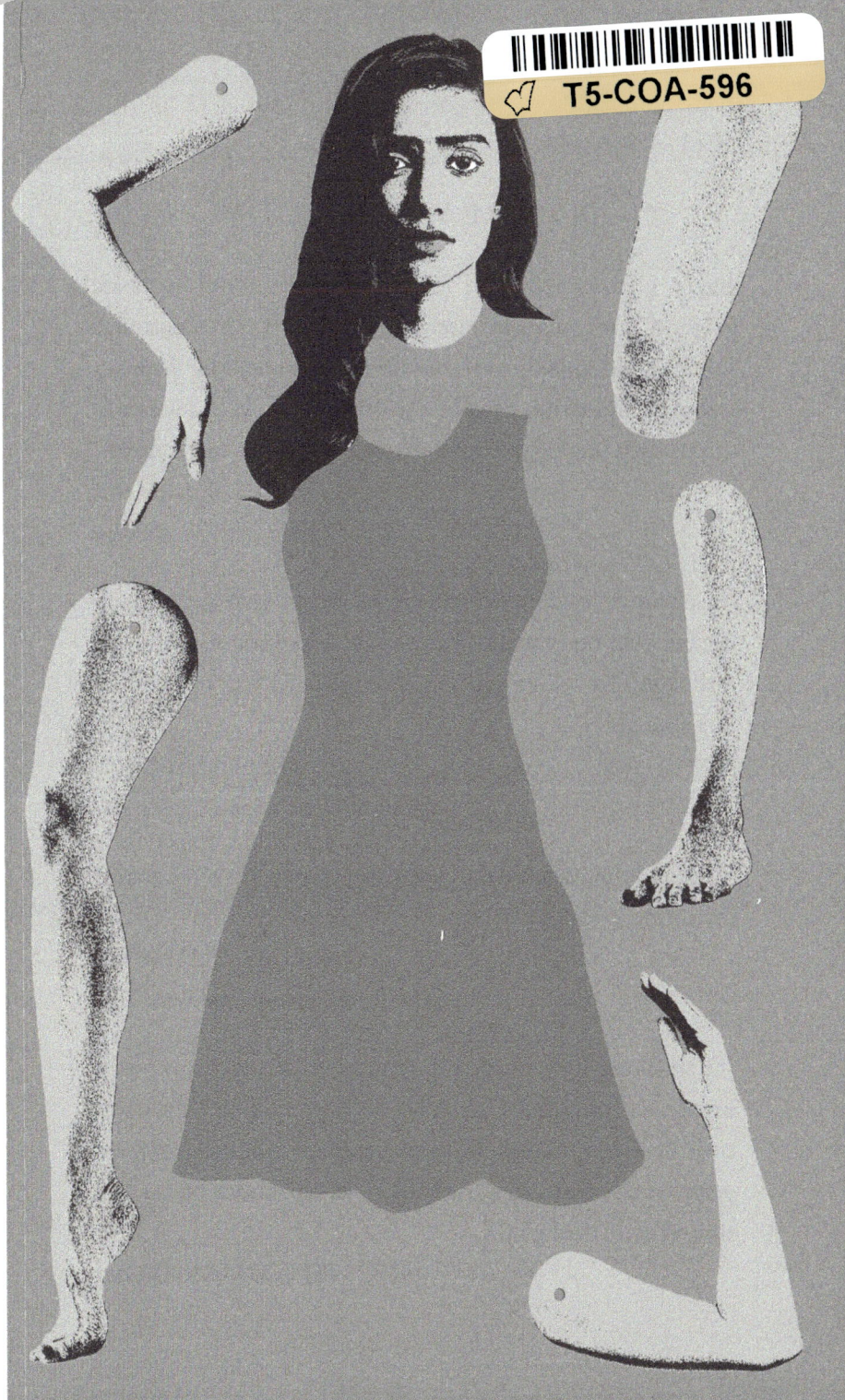

Praise for

MY DREADFUL BODY

"Egana Djabbarova's wild fever dream of a novel lays bare a world where female utterance is seismic, its eruption a shock of radicalizing violence. In prose marked by intimacy, restraint, and terror, *My Dreadful Body* introduces a writer of astounding intelligence and power. I could not put it down."

—HONOR MOORE,
author of *A Termination*

"An exquisite Bildungsroman by an exceptional author reading her own body as the bearer of inherited stigmas, offering a thought-provoking journey into what it's like to grow up as a stranger."

—SERGEI LEBEDEV,
author of *Oblivion* and *Untraceable*

"An extraordinary novel that translates corporality and estrangement into language."

—OLGA GRJASNOWA,
author of *All Russians Love Birch Trees*

"It's shocking how much the repression of women is based upon their physicality and also on how women themselves treat their own bodies. In language that's infinitely sensitive, gentle, and poetic, Egana Djabbarova recounts a brutal and sinister state of affairs."

—NORTH GERMAN RADIO

MY DREADFUL BODY

A NOVEL

EGANA DJABBAROVA

TRANSLATED FROM THE RUSSIAN
BY LISA C. HAYDEN

NEW VESSEL PRESS
NEW YORK

www.newvesselpress.com

Copyright © 2023 Egana Djabbarova and No Kidding Press
First published in Russian as
Руки женщин моей семьи были не для письма
Translation copyright © 2026 Lisa C. Hayden

All rights reserved. Except for brief passages quoted in a newspaper, magazine, radio, television, or website review, no part of this book may be reproduced in any form or by any means, electronic or mechanical, including photocopying and recording, or by any information storage and retrieval system, without permission in writing from the publisher.

LIBRARY OF CONGRESS CATALOGING-IN-PUBLICATION DATA
Djabbarova, Egana
[Ruki zhenshchin moei sem'i byli ne dlia pis'ma, English]
My Dreadful Body / Egana Djabbarova; translation by Lisa C. Hayden.
p. cm.
ISBN 978-1-954404-41-0

Library of Congress Control Number 2025940586
I. Russia—Fiction

To Grandfather and Bibi

> ...*A winding-sheet*
> *Is all the cover of his stainless form.*
> *Whom shall I clasp upon my bosom now?*
> —Hakim Ferdowsi

> *No one life is worthy of becoming the basis for a novel.*
> —Orhan Pamuk

> *My mother said: The darkness in my belly*
> *is the only darkness you command.*
> —Athena Farrokhzad

> *The past is never dead.*
> —William Faulkner

CONTENTS

I.	Eyebrows	3
II.	Eyes	12
III.	Hair	25
IV.	Mouth	38
V.	Shoulders	47
VI.	Hands	56
VII.	Tongue	67
VIII.	Back	78
IX.	Legs	90
X.	Throat	99
XI.	Belly	107

Translator's Note   119

# MY DREADFUL BODY

I
EYEBROWS

According to my mother's strict orders, the big, bushy black eyebrows in the oval mirror were not to be plucked. This was not just because Allah forbids his creatures from changing anything about their bodies. It was also because I was unmarried. The primary event in the life of any young Azerbaijani woman, after all, is undoubtedly her wedding and only that wedding can bestow the right to make changes, even if Allah does not approve of them. In small mountain settlements, the eyebrows were first and foremost in differentiating an innocent, unmarried young woman from a woman who had already married.

A married woman's eyebrows were even, almost artificial, and so thin they might have been drawn with ink to let people around them know that a girl was now forever a woman, that thick brows resembling paradisiacal shrubbery were in her past. Yes, most of the girls in a typical Russian school who admired themselves in tiny little round mirrors from state-run newsstands were perfectly calm when they used soulless metal tweezers to pluck unruly, bristly little hairs. I pondered for a long time what possible danger there could be in tweezing my eyebrows, given that the girls in my class were all still the same the next day, maybe even a little happier. My brows seemed to expand daily, occupying more and more space between my eyelids. If my girlfriends had something like pale vines, then I had the huge dark wings of a mountain bird.

The question of how to deal with my eyebrows preoccupied me just as much when we went to visit my father's relatives in Baku. Dense mattresses and coverlets of various colors, adorned with all kinds of decorations, lay, lazily stacked, on a bed in a small room. My aunts and grandmothers had filled most of those mattresses themselves. They first thoroughly washed lambswool, then carefully laid it out right in the yard, under the dazzling Baku sun, until the time came for the longest and most torturous part of assembly. Clean pillowcases decorated with roses were quickly filled with wool that Mama and Bibi, my aunt, packed in firmly, as if it were stuffing for a gutted turkey. They then sewed the edges by hand and pierced the center of the mattress with long stitches made by the very thickest and largest needles, which were so difficult and dangerous to use that they often covered the women's hands in bloody constellations. It was on those lovingly sewn and stacked mattresses that I sat with my cousins, silently observing how grown women with glistening rings on their fingers used silk thread to pull out each other's brows.

I recall wondering where their hands had mastered all those secret motions and how they'd learned to manipulate the thread so quickly and energetically that it flawlessly removed the unwanted while leaving the essential. The skin reddened quickly after recognizing the bitterness of loss, as if it mourned each tiny hair. Twenty minutes later, new brows had replaced the old, engraved on the skin like an ornament on a vase. Cold, calm, and unaware of their own past, those brows lent the face's owner a new expression unique to anyone acquainted with the strength of one's own willpower and the possibility of changing one's body. A childhood girlfriend had that same expression when we met on a hot Baku day after her wedding: she looked relieved because there was no longer any requirement to bear the heavy burden of innocence. In many situations, "it's finally allowed" had replaced the reproving "forbidden."

On the one hand, I liked interacting with my many cousins, aunts, and other relatives since they, after all, had grown up in and were living in a world with familiar rules. They understood what was impossible for me to explain to my classmates. On the other hand, they themselves had become the strictest protectresses of the rules once invented for them: if someone did something shameful or diverged from tradition, there was no doubt that everyone would find out about it, thanks to wagging tongues. This was why I couldn't admit to my cousins that I had a forbidden and rather sweet desire to pluck my eyebrows and why I secretly envied my classmates because they were able to make their own decisions about their bodies, unburdened by an endless set of interdictions.

After long deliberations I came to a decision: I swiped my mother's tweezers over the weekend and, unnoticed, plucked a couple of the most unpleasant and noticeable little hairs between my brows. And so the deed was done. The tweezers were returned to their original place and the little hairs that had fallen like autumn leaves were rinsed out of the smooth white sink. I experienced slight joy and now felt calmer when I was with my classmates and girlfriends, though pulling out the little hairs hadn't changed a thing. The world hadn't collapsed; my body wasn't cheapened. What kind of eyebrows did the women around me have? And why were they the way they were?

Even as a child, I knew for certain that I resembled my mother. It wasn't just photographs in family albums that testified to that: everyone who entered our home said the same thing. Peering for a couple of minutes, first at my childish face and then at my mother's, they'd joyfully conclude, "Just like Mama." I remember how it always amazed me that everyone so insistently sought that resemblance, as if it hadn't been preordained by the very facts of creation and birth. Maybe there was a question hidden in that desire to find resemblance, wondering if my mother's fate and my own would be as similar as our faces. Did a resemblance of faces result in a resemblance of fates? Were there similar fates for the heroines of Nizami Ganjavi's poems?

My eyebrows are all that I inherited from my father. A man's brows on a woman's face: strikingly defined black arches and, under each eyebrow, visible little hairs that looked like strewn tea leaves. Why did every woman in "Eastern" literature always have identical brows that looked like crescents and were as black as night? Why were only brows presumed to be black? What sort of eyebrows did Sheherazade have? Probably black ones.

My mother's eyebrows are black, too. They always seem a bit inquisitive, as if her brows pose a question every time she looks at me: Were you a worthy daughter today or not? Only rarely, usually at weddings, does she raise her eyebrows in joy. Weddings have always been her favorite events. Not just because they're still the primary way for the diaspora to socialize, particularly outside the motherland, but also because a wedding is a long-awaited opportunity to be outside the home, wear nice clothes, buy a new dress, put on makeup, pull out her favorite earrings and rings, gossip with girlfriends, and feel no shame when openly drinking a glass of wine. She loves weddings because there's no need to cook and she can forget all about her habitually difficult life, set aside cleaning, and simply be a part of the community. It was at a wedding that she met my father thirty years ago, though to be more exact, it was he who met her, which even more exactly means that he chose her over others. And of course one of the reasons he chose her was that she had thick, untouched eyebrows over eyes that occasionally watched the bride and groom dance. Could she have known that her modest, lowered gaze would elicit his loving feelings?

My maternal grandmother's eyebrows were just the same, though over time she'd completely stopped plucking them and they'd begun looking like an unkempt garden she loved more than other people. She viewed only her garden and her sewing machine with warmth and tenderness: it was as if she were caressing them because, unlike people, objects and plants never let her down. She cast people looks as dry and harsh as stale bread. You needed to prove your own usefulness in order to soften that gaze, which is why each summer everyone who ended up in her Georgian home was required to work throughout their stay by picking white and red cherries, harvesting and shelling hazelnuts, placing beans into large coarse bags to be sold, and gathering coriander and dill from the kitchen garden. No matter what you did, though, the gaze from under her sullen, grayed eyebrows remained the same: as calm and absent as solid ice.

My sister's gaze was just as perennially mean and serious. As those around us affirmed, she looked just like our father, with the exception of her bushy eyebrows, which she'd received from our mother. She inherited our grandmother's stern look: furrowed brows and a cold gaze. Even in a sweet photograph taken when she was one year old, two mean brown eyes are shining out from underneath firm, dense black curls. She was most envious of my eyebrows and often grieved, wondering why she'd inherited our mother's luxuriant brows that merged in the space between them, a place referred to with the lovely Latin word *glabella*. She was the one forced to suffer the most attacks from classmates (be they boys or girls), meaning she didn't hesitate for a second before buying her own metal tweezers so nobody would ever dare to mock her again.

Over time I forgot about the existence of my own eyebrows. Their width and thickness stopped bothering me, and I realized that eyebrows are comparable to life experience and cannot be identical. There is always something in them from the woman they belong to. They only began worrying me a couple of years later, in a cold, gray hospital corridor, where I was sitting in a long line of people whose bodies and faces were deformed, asymmetrical, and distorted. There was something inhuman in their faces, something larger than life. They showed so much suffering that I had to periodically sneak away for air in order to erase their faces from my mind with the tranquil blankness of a winter sky.

After sitting like that for two hours I imagined the neurologist had hidden away or died in his office. The door finally opened, though, and they began, little by little, letting people in. Inside, behind the door we'd longed for, sat the only neurologist in our region who injected muscle tissue with botulinum toxin. People left his office looking completely transformed: a woman with a wry neck emerged looking relieved and proudly carried away her beautiful, even, and long neck as if it were a banner; and a young man smiled, displaying the newfound symmetry of his facial muscles.

I joyfully rushed to the door when my turn finally came. I imagined my distorted face regaining its original appearance. And how two slivers of eyebrows—mutilated, their edges as uneven as a broken tea bowl, brought on by spasms of my facial muscles—would disappear after the return of eyebrows looking like a half-moon in the night sky or the arc of an arrow shot from a bow, and how I would proudly carry my newly restored face down the frozen street.

It was stuffy in the office. Everything was, as is usually the case in medical offices, either coldly blue or indifferently white. The doctor lowered his glasses a little, silently paged through my medical report, touched my shoulders, face, and hands, and calmly pre-empted me, "Botox won't help you, too much has been affected." I kept sitting, incapable of standing and leaving without the promised miracle, but then he unassumingly opened the door and nodded slightly.

Half a year before that, it was my eyebrows that enabled another neurologist to make a diagnosis. This was yet another trip to see a doctor from whom I expected nothing. Not one doctor had been able to answer the question of what was happening to my body or why I couldn't control my arm and leg muscles, so the majority lazily concluded "stress" or "psychosomatic" and pushed me out the door before they even had time to close their yawning mouths. The day I saw this doctor, I'd firmly decided that I'd go to the psychiatric unit if he said it was psychosomatic.

The doctor was young, seemingly under forty, and his large body and thick beard immediately calmed me. I knew he wouldn't make a mistake. He filled out paperwork and then began examining me, asking me to raise and then lower my eyebrows and to smile, but his own warm and even smile suddenly turned to alarm; he quickly grabbed my file and went off somewhere. When he returned, he said I needed to come back at eight the next morning so we could see the department head. And that's how my black eyebrows answered my question. They no longer served as a frame or decoration for my face, they no longer symbolized purity and innocence, and they had ceased being genetic happenstance. They were now harbingers of tremendous misfortune, a red flare on the high seas. Someone who could interpret all this had finally appeared.

11
EYES

ALL THE POPULAR GIRLS IN MY CLASS at school had blue or green eyes, so I quickly realized I was unlucky that my own eyes were brown. There was nothing interesting about them: they were as ordinary as tree bark, the top of a sturdy table, or a cleaning lady's floor rag. Too many ugly and common things were brown. All my cousins and other relatives also had brown eyes. That's nothing like a blue sky or roaring blue ocean or lovely green leaves or exciting green grass or fabulous blue rivers. Why was everything beautiful either blue or green? Why was there so little that was beautiful and brown?

It turned out that the Earth had been poisoned to its very core after the decaying bodies of former colonizers managed to pass on their standards to the world, whereby everything blue was beautiful but brown was hideous. So that even a little girl from a world where everyone else has brown eyes wanted blue eyes. Blue ones like some of the sultans' wives or Turkish actresses had, probably after receiving the blueness from mothers, grandmothers, and great-grandmothers who were in the sultans' harems or became trophies for the conquering Ottoman Empire. In my Baku cousins' stuffy apartments, we watched beguiling Turkish videos: we saw the blue eyes of Turkish actresses or pop singers, sadly noting that our bloodlines had no such eyes. Since my sister and I didn't speak Azerbaijani well and our cousins didn't speak Russian, we had no common conversation topics, meaning all we could do together was look. We looked at objects, rooms, books, and the television screen. In essence, we wanted to rewrite the history of our bloodline so that distant blue-eyed beauties appeared in it after having been enslaved because of their attractiveness and atypical appearances. The ordeal of the violence that had occurred would thus turn us into something unusual, setting us apart from the crowd and placing us in the company of other beautiful girls. But why had beauty ended up being inseparable from violence? And why did one woman need to enslave another in order to become "the norm"?

At some point, I became utterly preoccupied with the idea of changing my eye color from brown. I was sad when I paged through photos in magazines where the actresses and models (of course) had blue eyes, and I was sad when I observed my blue-eyed classmates. I decided that I definitely had to transform my own eyes by growing up and buying the bluest contact lenses possible so my eyes would finally stop being brown. Even if they didn't turn blue, I wanted them at least to look like my father's eyes, which were honey brown with greenish flecks. My eyes stayed brown no matter how much I attempted to convince myself that they weren't or tried applying makeup after choosing an essential shade of eyeshadow. One time, though, I suddenly burst into tears while sitting in front of a mirror. And when I looked at my reflection, I noticed that my eyes had become a bit lighter and taken on a honey tint along with green, like my father's eye color, though mine was fainter, nearly unnoticeable. I finally calmed down: my eyes weren't completely brown after all, and they did have a greenish tint, though the truth was that the change only appeared after many tears. My eyes only lightened during moments of despair, as if suffering were a bleach, the price to be paid for the "beautiful."

Even a household's *göz monjuk*—or, the eye of Satan, as some imams call it—was blue. It was an important attribute of any Azerbaijani home: a blue eye with a small black pupil in the middle. It hung over the entrance to prevent any member of the family from falling under the evil eye; children wore pins with little beads that looked like eyes, too. The eye of Satan also hung across from the entrance to small stores and local artists' studios in Baku's *İçərişəhər*, the Old City. I remember from early childhood that the scariest thing a stranger could do was cast the evil eye on someone, which is why all the women in my family knew several methods for protecting themselves and their loved ones. In addition to the little eyes, there was also *uzerlik*[1], a plant that made a house a home. As soon as the last guest closed the door behind

---

1 Узерлик, transliterated into Russian from the Azeri *üzərlik*, is the plant known in English as wild rue.

them, my mother would take out a generous bunch of *uzerlik* and burn it in a special vessel. It's so intoxicating, dense, and intriguing that I've never sensed a more pleasant and interesting smell in my whole life. There was no place safer in the entire world than a dense cloud of *uzerlik*: my mother would shroud you in smoke and intone, "*Pis gozler partasin pis gozler kor olsun.*"[2] My mother maintained that haters' eyes burst each time a dry head of the *uzerlik* broke off. The evil eye explained nearly any unhappiness in a home and was to blame for any calamity that came about. It didn't matter if eyes were blue or brown—the main thing was if they were kind or evil. And that they wanted beauty to be beautiful and health to be healthy.

We always returned to Russia from summer vacation with a multitude of little eyes, be they in bracelets on slender wrists or on safety pins and chains with beads. I enthusiastically put on blue bracelets, shrewdly thinking that they'd protect me if someone wished me ill. The little blue amulets helped me forget my own eye color and reminded me to always look instead into the eyes of others. Mama had brown eyes, as did my sister, my mother's mother, my mother's sister, and my girl cousins: everyone around me had brown eyes.

For me, though, it was my paternal grandmother who had the most mysterious eyes. Black-and-white photographs in albums and on a large gravestone didn't convey the color of her eyes, something my father never spoke about. Of

---

[2] "May the eyes of ill-wishers burst, may evil eyes go blind" (Azerbaijani).

course it's easy to guess that they were brown, just like all her children's eyes. But something else was more important: they radiated kindness. One year when my sister and I were in Baku for our usual summer visit, Mama, Papa, and my uncle were all very serious and sad as we rode somewhere. The ride was long, almost an hour, before we saw large gray and sand-colored gravestones. All kinds of people stared at us from those stones, looking quite alive: some peered at us thoughtfully, some with sorrow, some with smiles. We walked past unknown others until we came to a fence, behind which were three faces: Papa's mother, Papa's father, and Papa's grandmother (now four, with the addition of Papa's sister). The grown-ups began crying. Papa and my uncle were like little boys, leaning helplessly against the gravestone, wiping their tears, and tenderly stroking the stone's angled edge as if it were a maternal shoulder. The graves were completely overgrown with grass since the adult children came only once a year, and even that was difficult given that they were scattered around various countries and cities. My uncle decided to burn the grass, which caught fire instantly so everything quickly flared up: my grandparents looked reproachfully at their eldest son, who had been too lazy to remove the grass by hand. My sister and I leaned against a little gate and watched the flame blaze brighter and brighter, bringing the dead and the living closer together.

Only my grandmother's eyes stayed the same: it was as if they shone, still retaining a love undiminished as long as she lived. I never saw her other than in old photographs, but

I know she was one of those people whose love never fades. She had big eyes, a beauty mark near her lips, dimples in her cheeks, and hair that hung past her hips; she wore long braids until the end of her days, though caring for them was not at all easy. She needed to place a big metal basin in the middle of a room, fill the basin with heated water, set a stool next to it, and then, partially bending, pour water from a ladle to wash her hair. Braiding and unbraiding her long, thick, black hair was the most difficult part. My father's mother was the reason our father forbade us to cut our braids: they needed to be long because only long hair was considered beautiful.

My grandmother rose at five each morning so she could go to prepare breakfast for her mother, who lived five minutes away from the house where my grandparents lived. She paid for those outings with her body: every trip out of the house turned into another bruise, evidence of her husband's rage, because he thought all the men nearby would lust after his wife. If he noticed a random man gaze at his wife, that evening she would dab at her face, belly, and back with dampened fabric as dense and black as the night itself. Nothing calmed Baba, my grandfather, who even died looking at his wife's photograph; he observes her after her death, too. They now lie alongside one another: his mean, cold eyes tensely track every passerby as she looks lovingly at the little gate, awaiting her children, who are her main consolation and her only joy.

I wonder why an Eastern woman's eyes needed to be as black and bottomless as the Kaaba in Mecca. Why should a woman's eyes be bottomless? And able only to accommodate the world, having no right to change it. Does the world really exist when someone's eyes are closed?

Did the evil eye cause me to stop growing and cause my body to start falling apart? I thought illness would rob me of only the biggest things, but it also affected my eyesight: one day I woke up and realized the world had slowed. It was as if someone had changed the playback speed, space had been ripped to pieces like an unsent love letter, and the world was collapsing. A neurologist solved the mystery. It turned out that my pupil was twitching and jerking, as if it had forgotten how it was supposed to move. The world seemed torn, sluggish, and very blurry without glasses, meaning I could only make out major details and bright spots.

My vision had been poor since childhood, so my mother dragged me to eye doctors and bought all kinds of glasses, starting with black pinhole glasses and ending with corrective lenses. The only thing I was allowed to eat in huge quantities was bilberries, which were good for the eyes and darkened my mouth purple for several days, showing what I'd eaten. We tested every available device for the eyes, including synoptophores and an old machine that treated squinting. I obediently made weekly trips to the pediatric ophthalmologist, where I sat on an uncomfortable couch and used my eyes to connect a cat and its tail, the top and bottom of a holiday tree, a star, an airplane, and a missile. I went to the other end of the city to look at colored dots and spots strewn on a screen. My vision was still deteriorating, though, and becoming less dependable and distinct with each day. I got glasses very early. My first pair had red frames and a leopard-patterned case with a black microfiber cloth to wipe the lenses. I liked wearing them because my face changed noticeably. I looked older and I could see the world the same way everyone else did: distinctly. My second pair of glasses lasted longest of all and were ugly. I don't remember why we chose them, but maybe it was because they were inexpensive, with two square lenses in dark-red frames. Unattractive glasses spoiled my adolescence: I was already the first girl to get beaten up because I was a nerd and the target of unutterable slurs. And then came the hideous red glasses. Unlike my girlfriends and others around me, however, my glasses—like books—never betrayed me. They always waited for me to return to their world when I opened up another book or took them off my nightstand; they waited for me to open my eyes again.

Not many children wore glasses, but every four-eyes nodded understandingly when making eye contact with their brothers and sisters in suffering and curiously eyeing the others' alien accessories. It's interesting that I was the lone child in our large family to wear glasses. That was why Bibi firmly decided the books were to blame, since I read too many of them. Everyone in my family had excellent vision, so it remains unclear who passed bad eyes along to me.

Mama sometimes attempted to force me to wear contact lenses, particularly if we were going to yet another wedding. Weddings, after all, weren't simply prime entertainment but also an opportunity to put a mature and marriageable daughter on display for the Azeri diaspora community. Everyone dressed up, not just festively but as if this were the last feast before the end of the world. A family's entire collection of gold jewelry was displayed on the daughter and nobody begrudged money for beautiful hairdos, makeup, or floor-length dresses. The dresses needed to shimmer and catch the eye, but remain demure. Cleavage and beautiful breasts had to be hidden; so did long legs. The body was allowed to be exhibited, so it was clear to everyone that the woman was not only youthful and healthy but innocent. Each time we prepared for a wedding, my mother would start entreating me to finally stop wearing my glasses and use contacts at least once in my life so I could be a little prettier.

The longer she insisted, though, the more unwilling I was to stop wearing glasses. What stung most about her persistence and the local wedding ritual was that the women in that odd, festive, and flashy world remained commodities. Every parent considered it their duty to present their daughter in the best light possible, and so the adults sat at the table, bragging to one another about their children's successes at school and in academic competitions, their excellent grades, and their ability to cook national dishes. Children were the main topic of discussion. These conversations were initially about school achievements, but new topics emerged as the children grew up: who was engaged, who was accepted to what university, who married when, who divorced when, and, of course, who got out of control. The ones who (in the community's opinion) went off the rails were subjected to the most blistering and extended discussions: mouths puckered as if they were sucking marrow out of bones, eyebrows rose in surprise while awaiting the particulars, and fingers nervously kept track of each detail of an unworthy biography.

I liked beautiful traditional dances, *plov* dishes made with rice, and white bridal dresses, but I started avoiding weddings. I didn't want to feel like a commodity whose value was speculated upon by adults seated at an opulent table. The servers needed to move the dishes closer and closer together to make space for more: grilled salad, *lobio*, *khashlama* made with lamb and beef, dolmas, royal plov, and kebabs. The head table smelled fragrant thanks to cut flowers and gifted bouquets, and a blinding massive chandelier hung from the ceiling. Each time I walked into the ballroom, I immediately sensed the tenacious, curious gazes of men and women directed at my body. They were all rating how I was dressed, how I was made up, the length of my skirt, how my hair looked, how I spoke and smiled, and whether I was drinking wine. And (if drinking wine) how many glasses.

In the world where I grew up, gazes penetrated every little corner. The evil eye, the neighbors' eyes, the relatives' eyes, the random pedestrian's eyes, the unscrupulous men's eyes, the women's unhappy eyes. Life in the community was reminiscent of a reality show with constant video surveillance: no action, word, or undertaking went unnoticed.

The first thing my mother told us as soon as we learned to walk, and were able to step across the threshold of our parents' home, was that everything has eyes. We must always look after ourselves, noting how others see us, since we're not just our father's beloved children but also his capital, his reputation, his honor, and his face. In this world, even when apart from him, you not only always carry his surname and patronymic (it's no coincidence that the majority of Turkic patronymics contain the word *kızı*, "daughter," and *oğlu*, "son," in the proper order) but you are a daughter until your very death and you are a son who represents the family line. And Allah help you if you do something that darkens your parents' joy and disgraces your family line. After all, the community is prepared to protect you as long as you are its worthy representative, but it will destroy you just as readily if you disobey. It could not be otherwise. The East and the West have never come to resemble one another: Telegonus kills Ulysses, Rostam kills Sohrab, and father kills son because only he is given the right. He gives life and he takes it away.

Of course the most frightening eyes belong to my father: I always knew he was capable of taking my life if it didn't suit him. I love him but have always feared him, and I fear him as much as I love him. My father's frightening eyes scared my sister and me more than all the monsters in the world. Especially when we were children, when he drank a lot. Every evening, he'd put a faceted tumbler in front of himself and fill it to the very brim with Russian Standard vodka. And then my father would drink until his warm eyes flecked with honey and green became black and bloody, just like his own father's eyes. We would see that change and await his rage. His dangerous hands with thick tendons and veins instantly grew longer and overturned tables, smashed all the dishes in the house, smashed a solid cutting board into two even pieces over my mother's head, and beat my mother, who became as small as the pebbles at the seaside. My mother pressed all of herself into the floor, tightly closing her eyes and waiting for the end of his raging storm. Initially we couldn't interfere because we were little and we froze. We looked through a tiny crack between the door and the jamb, and our eyes registered his rage as his fists taught us the most important rule of the house, to never anger our father. Each of his strikes at our mother's powerless body drove our freedom into the grave, hammering his words deeper and deeper, flinging our hopes like dirt, and using his big feet to tamp our little bodies into a box labeled "woman."

A woman is not supposed to speak, a woman is not supposed to contradict, and a woman is not allowed to forget that she is an object in a sentence rather than its main subject. But the primary thing that his fists taught us was to keep silent, to lock away our dreams and wishes, and to never tell anyone our dark secrets.

Only men were allowed to look someone in the eye or to look with rage or lust. Nothing prevented young men at Azerbaijani markets from looking me over from head to toe: their eyes undressed every woman on the street, imagining her body, possessing her body. One hot day I noticed that heavy, carnivorous, poisonous gaze when we went to the flea market. I was about thirteen and I defiantly turned toward the brazen observer and looked him right in the eye. That didn't stop him from continuing to devour me with his eyes, though, so I walked up to him and hit him in the face. And that provoked loud outbursts from other merchants and customers. It seems that was when Bibi realized that I would cause only problems because I was unable to lower my eyes and keep my mouth shut.

III

HAIR

My mother always wanted to have a son—then again, all the women in our family always wanted to have sons. Of course, their daughters brought them happiness, but daughters were merely temporary inhabitants of the home and were nurtured for other families, for their future husbands' families. The main thing any little girl should do was marry and leave the parental home to the sounds of "Vagzaly."[3] A daughter unable to make her parents happy with her marriage was considered a bad daughter.

My mother wanted a son, but her hair began falling out after he was finally born. A small bald spot, initially almost unnoticeable and easy to cover by combing over, expanded with time, destroying all of my mother's beautiful thick black hair. It fell out in clumps, then grew back as strange and curly gray hair that also quickly fell out. It was odd to see this new, unfamiliar mother—a tired woman attempting in vain

---

3 *Вагзалы* ("Vagzly" if transliterated to English) is the Russian transliteration of the Azerbaijani *Vağzalı*. It is the title of a song traditionally played when seeing a bride off from her father's home. It is also a folk dance for weddings. The title translates to "train station" since, in the past, a bride often left her parents' home for the groom's home by train.

to save her remaining strands of hair—because she wasn't the same mother who had beautiful long black hair in childhood photos. Mama frantically collected all the hair-growth home remedies on the Internet, rubbed mixtures of onion and garlic and castor oil onto her scalp, went for painful injections, and took vitamins, but nothing helped. Her hair was gone, taking her youth, her beauty, and her past along with it. Instead of remedies, shampoos, and creams for hair loss, she now had a multitude of headscarves as well as a genuine wig that she could barely wear, complaining that her head itched and sweated underneath. It's possible her hair was the price paid for her long-awaited healthy son, a late and beloved little boy with puffy lips and long lashes. Though she was sad to lose the black hair that preserved the memory of all the worthy women of the family line—each of whom, of course, had long hair—the little boy she had wished for over the years was some consolation.

Back when we were children, my sister and I knew that any self-respecting little girl should have long, long hair that makes it easy to hide the contours of maturing and changing bodies, hair whose length conveyed its wearer's patience and humility. Long hair also differentiated girls from boys, which is why as a schoolgirl I had very long hair, below my waist, and usually plaited it into a fat braid instead of wearing it loose. Of course hardly anyone admired my long hair: it wasn't exciting and it was just bothersome for me since it was impossible to deal with if I didn't braid it or gather it up in a high bun. That was why I soon had another dream: cutting my hair. I secretly looked at pictures of short haircuts in magazines, saving photos of actresses I liked and attempting to imagine which haircut would flatter me most. I needed my father's permission to cut my hair, but of course he was against it.

The day did come, though, when I went off to a hair salon and had my hair cut to shoulder length without asking anyone. That was also the day I finally left the hospital. It was a nice March day, albeit slippery outside, so I stepped carefully, leaning on my cane. After being released, I went to fulfill a promise I'd made to myself: I would cut my hair when I was able to speak again.

Two weeks before that, I'd gone to my second job, where I suddenly sensed that something was wrong with my foot. I felt it dragging on the ground and couldn't place it evenly, no matter how hard I tried. By the time I entered the classroom, my foot had turned into a pirate's wooden leg that hardly bent, meaning I had to drag it behind me. My hands weren't responding either and I could barely pick up a marker; my fingers shook and flung things. After lessons ended and all the children left the classroom, I realized my right arm was becoming wooden, too. When I made it home, I lay on the bed and closed my eyes. I thought I'd be able to fall asleep, but my body resembled willow branches gone mad from a strong wind. My arms and legs kept twitching, my muscles cramped and spasmed, and I was scared. Thinking it might be a stroke, I called an ambulance. The ambulance came forty minutes later and the medic confidently walked into the room and asked my name. I answered her, but everything immediately went icy cold inside me. There were only two of us in the room—the paramedic and I—which meant I was the one speaking, but not in my own voice. It was a strange, metallic voice. Based on the doctor's perplexed gaze, I realized she hadn't been able to make out my name. My speech sounded like a jumble of inarticulate sounds that I could barely force out.

It was only at that moment that I began to feel truly frightened: I realized that something irreversible was happening to my body, something I couldn't control, something bigger than me.

Following protocol, the doctors brought me to the closest hospital, though it looked abandoned, making it difficult to identify. Plaster was coming down inside, there were old wheelchairs all over, and the furniture didn't seem to have been replaced since the hospital had opened. A sweet woman at the reception desk kindly wondered if we should take the stairs or the elevator. When she met my scowl, she decided to use the creaking old elevator after all, though it let out frightening sounds as it rose, slowing threateningly at each floor as if it were contemplating whether to let people out or leave them in its belly. We finally reached the neurology department, where metal handrails led right into the wards. My displeased roommates rubbed their eyes upon being woken up, but after noticing my fear and determining my age, they spontaneously set to helping me put my blanket into the duvet cover and stuff my pillow into a pillowcase.

I woke up in the morning when a neurologist poked me with a needle. As before, my speech sounded unfamiliar and the neurologist asked me to repeat the same tongue twister every day: *the three hundred thirty-third artillery brigade.* Each syllable was very difficult for me, as if my throat was being squeezed in a vise, and the sounds didn't come out of my mouth on their own as usual: I now needed to force each muscle to work. I gloomily wondered how I'd be able to lead my course on Russian phonetics for foreigners if I couldn't even utter a line from a Tsvetaeva poem or my own name.

They did an MRI the next day, albeit as a paid service and at a different hospital, since this one only had X-ray equipment. Evening was already falling when we got into the ambulance and drove off: streetlamps lit the way, oblivious to how frightening they were for people in ambulances. We arrived at the empty hospital, where a radiologist was unhappily chewing her supper, and then went to a small room where a nurse repeated three times that I needed to take off everything metallic. She then led me to a large, strange machine and told me to lie down. The interior of the white machine was unusual: its form reminded me of a coffin or an oven for cremation, as if a flame would be lit at any moment and fire would consume my malfunctioning body. The machine clanged and let out horrible, guttural sounds as it transferred my brain's secrets to someone facing it. Sitting in the hallway, awaiting the results, I thought about how small hospital spaces actually were. It was as if all of them—MRI machines, X-ray machines that confine you to a strictly regimented space, the chronically crowded wards, the horribly narrow hallways, and even the exam room, where your area is limited to a chair opposite the doctor—were preparing you for a coffin.

The MRI showed strange lesions that could have been the result of birth trauma but could also be evidence of illness. The doctors were clearly perplexed and didn't understand what was happening to me or how to treat me, so they ultimately surmised that it was multiple sclerosis and started pumping large doses of prednisolone into me. My body plumped up from the prednisolone and I became very mean. Everything irritated me: how people walked, how they breathed, and how slowly time dragged in the ward. For some reason, five reproductions of Orthodox icons hung over my bed, forming a cross. I read books in the ward and wandered down the hallway to stretch my legs, walking as far as a metal door that read *Chapel*. The doors there were always tightly closed, but a light scent of incense wafted from behind them.

Days passed but the diagnosis remained unknown, so they released me after writing "multiple sclerosis" with a question mark. The night before my discharge, the neurologist looked at my neck and suspected that the issue was with my muscles; they were rock-hard and that had apparently led to dysarthria. She rummaged around in a desk drawer and took out Mydocalm. "Let's try an experiment. Maybe it will help," she said, handing me two white pills. I took the medicine and went to the ward. I chatted with my roommate and she suddenly asked me, in surprise, "Do you hear that? You're talking normally!" That's how we ascertained that Mydocalm helped me talk. It restored my speech and I made a haircut appointment that same day.

I was scared: I'd never cut my hair and was afraid I was committing a crime against all the women of my family line, destroying the memory of the ancestors who endured in my hair. At the same time, I was very tired of long hair because I constantly needed to do something with it—wash it, comb it, braid it, put it up in a bun—and that required daily effort. The longer it grew, the more effort was required. Not to mention that it was heavy, so my neck started aching from the weight by the end of a long day.

My paternal grandmother mourned for a long time after she had to cut her hair in a small room, under the intent gaze of the Azerbaijani sun: as she slowly brought the blades of her scissors together, the heavy locks fell into a metal basin. She knew that her history would no longer continue given that she was dying of cancer, which had already destroyed her fragile kidneys. Her honor, which she had borne throughout her long life, was left, helpless, lying at the bottom of the metal basin. She could no longer care for her hair and had no desire to ask for someone else's help, since tending to it is a woman's task.

My maternal grandmother mourned for a long time after she had to cut her hair in a small room, under the intent gaze of the Georgian sun: as she brought the blades of her scissors together, the heavy locks fell to the wooden floor of the house that her hands once built. She knew that her history would no longer continue given that she was dying of cancer, which had already destroyed her fragile kidneys.

I did not mourn at all when the local hairdresser's large metal scissors cut my long hair, taking along with it the story of my past and my healthy body, which would never be the same. When I went home, my mother just remarked sadly that it was better before; my father said nothing and turned toward the wall in disappointment. None of us knew then that three years later my remaining hair would also end up cropped.

It was an abnormally hot Russian summer when a diagnosis was finally made three years later. I was lying in Ward 512 of the neurology department with yet another IV, observing my roommates. Our ward was considered rough: three patients had secondary progressive multiple sclerosis and I had chorea of unknown origin. We were all characterized by an utter lack of optimism and the presence of canes beside our beds, as well as something we learned one day during daily rounds: we were all unable to pass the Romberg test.

Everything changed at eight o'clock one morning when the young neurologist and I went to the department head's office, where he sat at his desk and carefully observed as I attempted to drag my right foot to the chair. As soon as I sat down he said he had four theories of what was happening, although he had only seen the fourth a couple of times during his forty years of practice. Using assessments and experimental treatment, he'd been able to make a diagnosis, which turned out to be the fourth possibility: generalized dystonia. He was honest and immediately filled me in on all of the disease's defining traits, warning me that over time practically all of the muscles become implicated. He also admitted that nobody fully knows how and why dystonia comes about. He prescribed treatment including, among other things, daily clonazepam, which was to be administered at strictly set hours that a nurse wrote down in a special log, along with the dosage. I didn't need to wait long for side effects: my sense of balance seemed to have disappeared forever and I fell all the time. I fell in the hospital basement, where everyone went to smoke and chat about life, in the elevator, and in the yard; everything around me seemed to spin like a windmill's blades; my body was soft, pliant, and absolutely unresponsive. The situation didn't improve after a year of treatment: the illness was progressing and become even more aggressive. It was difficult to get around without a cane because my foot clenched as if it was wearing an invisible pointe shoe, making every step painful. The right side of my neck was bent double and I couldn't straighten it without myorelaxants. My muscles contracted constantly and uncontrollably, becoming ironlike rocks. I started waking up with horrible back spasms that caused pain unlike any I'd known before, as if an entire crowd of men were kicking me. Every time I woke up meant a new cycle of pain, new spasms, new cramps, and yet another rock-hard muscle.

One day I caught myself thinking that I didn't want to wake up—that I wanted to die. It was then that they referred me for botulinum toxin therapy, though they didn't end up doing the treatment because it turned out to be too late since too many muscles were affected. The only remaining option was an operation with a name I didn't know: deep brain stimulation. After learning the name of the procedure, I went off to google it and read scientific articles, watch YouTube videos, and read patients' testimonials. The procedure looked like something fantastical: they stitch a small device under the collarbone and thread a wire through the neck to connect it to electrodes in the brain so the device can send healing electrical impulses to the right places. Patients saw dramatic changes that resembled miracles unfolding before a live camera. A man with Parkinson's was confidently playing the violin after implantation of a stimulator, and a woman with an essential tremor disorder could firmly hold small objects in her hand. Of course I knew the risks and understood that the procedure couldn't help in all cases. In order to have the procedure, I spent a long time methodically gathering documents to confirm that I needed the operation even if I couldn't afford it. I was then placed on a list for government funding and went to the Federal Center of Neurosurgery for a consultation, where the entire department had gathered to see a severe case of generalized dystonia.

I was assigned a long (fourteen-digit) number—65.0000.02606.189—that I needed to enter on the Ministry of Health site to track my status. I went there every day for a year, entered the number, which I'd learned by heart, and saw the same text:

> Profile 08.00
> G54.8
> 65.0000.02606.189
> [under review]

When they finally called me, a woman's voice quickly and almost mechanically announced that they expected me on November 16 at the Federal Center, that someone ahead of me had declined an operation and I was next in line. The following two weeks flew by, as if I'd closed my eyes for a minute then reopened them after having successfully endured the defense of my dissertation, taken a vacation without pay, done necessary research, lost my mind from paranoia because I was terrified of getting sick, packed my things for the operation, and met with friends... And then the night came when my father and I got in the car and drove off. The Center of Neurosurgery is in Tyumen, so we had a four-hour drive, during which I periodically fell asleep and woke up to Azerbaijani songs that my father always listens to at full volume in the car.

I never lost the sense of the unreality of what was happening: it seemed as if this wasn't my life, that it couldn't be my life. Outside the car window, the vast, expansive wintry steppe was as uniform as a sleeping woman's calm breath; there were neither buildings nor stores. A generous layer of snow covered the ground and the treetops, tractor trailers lumbered past, and my father sighed each time because at one point he'd dreamed of being a truck driver, a long-distance trucker. He liked the idea of constant motion and travel, so he was always content with a long trip ahead.

When we arrived, I started thinking that maybe I wouldn't go in, maybe this illness would pass on its own, abandoning my body as quickly as it had arrived. On the other hand, I thought, if the operation goes well, I can live without pain, I can wake up without yet more cramps. Curiosity won out, so we took the elevator up to the neurology department. The department was very nice, newly renovated, and almost shiny. Solid metal handrails adorned the edges of white walls and a big black couch surrounded by plants and a couple of small icons stood alongside the nurses' station, ready to care for patients by cheering them up as they walked past. I was led to a large ward for two people, though there was no other patient; my father left. And so I remained, completely alone, in the middle of a wintry expanse filled with the unknown.

It was very quiet in the department and all I could hear was the metallic sound of hair clippers. People with freshly shaved heads periodically walked down the hallway; some had only been half-shaved. I quickly learned that the sound of the clippers meant I'd hear the knocking of stretcher wheels the next morning because heads were shaved the night before operations.

The third day arrived and nothing had happened. I'd started to think I'd just come for a short visit until one night a nurse told me to go to the nurses' station. We went together to a procedure room covered in sheets of plastic for easy cleanup; she asked me to sit on a chair in the middle of the room. I immediately realized the nurse was going to shave my head. She took the clipper, turned it on, and drew it right down the middle of my head, from my forehead to the nape of my neck. "Well then, now I need to shave it all," she said cheerfully. The metallic tip of the clipper quickly slid over my head, baring an oddly-shaped skull with a multitude of scars. I'd known they'd shave my hair, known that would be unavoidable, but for some reason I burst into tears the moment I looked at the reflection of my shorn scalp.

That was it. My past, the past of all the women in my family, the memory of my ancestors, the history of a single body—all that now lay on the cold floor. I'd known I would never be part of the past, known I could never live as before, known I would never plait long braids as my grandmothers had. A completely different fate lay ahead of me.

IV
MOUTH

THE MOUTH WAS NOT INTENDED FOR SPEAKING. None of the women around me ever said what they genuinely wanted to say and none interrupted men's conversations—a woman wasn't supposed to do that. The mouth was needed to taste food that had been prepared, to consume food, to lull children to sleep, to lay down rules.

Food was the most important thing in the world of the women I knew. They shared recipes with one another, generously served up plov with a crispy, greasy crust, and gave each other dolmas and homemade baklava. Mouths were to be kept shut, though all the women in my family had mouths that were capable of speaking.

My maternal grandmother's lips were always firmly pursed, as if she was angry and wasn't allowing words to escape. She was taciturn and barely spoke with any of us. She addressed me twice.

The first time, she said only one word to me: *ilan*. I was standing in the kitchen garden, gathering herbs, when I suddenly heard the loud and distinct word *snake*. My grandmother's hand pointed to the soil next to me and I looked down to see a long red snake crawling through the grass.

She and I didn't speak at all the rest of the time. She was a seamstress, not just any seamstress but the principal seamstress in a small Georgian village. She sewed clothes for practically all the women in the area and she had full trunks of handmade lace napkins and beautiful white pillowcases embroidered in the satin stitch. All day long, the sound of her sewing machine, its pedal rhythmically hitting the floor, emerged from behind the closed door of her room.

My grandmother's trunks were always filled with towels, napkins, tablecloths, ladies' jackets, skirts, and nightgowns. Women came to my grandparents' house every morning— neighbors, relatives, women from afar, women who'd heard recommendations—and each brought a laboriously handwritten list of wishes. The main and first point on each woman's list was, of course, *dzhekhiz*, a dowry gathered from childhood and consisting of gifts from relatives. Everyone, without exception, asked for the most beautiful sheets, pillowcases, and coverlets for their daughters, the future brides. They took their time assessing each stitch on a napkin, attempting to find flaws in my grandmother's embroidery so they could get hold of a vest or new dress at a discount, though that didn't work with her. She coldly shook her head and wordlessly pulled the clothing out of the dissatisfied women's hands. She had no need to beg the customers: she knew the price of every stitch on the fabric and knew for certain that if this woman wouldn't buy it, another one would. After realizing the rules of the game, her customers strove to find the most beautiful items faster than others and, most importantly, to buy them. The trunk with children's clothing was particularly revered because it held the undershirts, swaddling clothes, and children's hats that were cherished attributes of impending motherhood and a carefree old age: everyone in the village knew that children are like walking sticks that would be worth the expense over time.

Only after her death did I learn that there was something in the trunk for me, too: a yellow vest with large buttons. I wondered why she had decided to leave that particular item for me. Why not a dress or a skirt? I've always asked myself that question but have never been able to answer it.

When I heard her voice the second time, she wasn't speaking to me. She was delirious on the other side of a wall, arguing with my grandfather. She already knew she was dying, knew she had very little time left, and was enraged, shouting curses and vowing to my grandfather that she wouldn't give him life from the other side if he dared bring another woman into this house. She panicked when she thought of how he might love someone else, that some other woman would touch her trunks and her beloved sewing machine, and walk around the house she'd built with her own hands. After she died, it became even quieter in the house than before. Neighbors trickled into the yard to share their condolences. It was on that day—the day we parted with her—that I tried something my mouth will never forget. It was funeral halva, which was bright orange, sweet, and very delicious, the most delicious food I'd ever eaten. I'd never experienced as much shame as that day: How could I enjoy something that was directly associated with my grandmother's death? I kept eating that halva, making my hands greasy and sticky, but I just couldn't eat enough of it. Women's sobbing was audible inside and it seemed as if the house itself were weeping, mourning her departure.

I never saw my paternal grandmother's mouth, but I knew that she had never contradicted her husband, right up until her death: all her words were turned into deeds, into the foods she cooked, the laundry, the sewing. Her words were *shekarbura*,[4] thin *kutaby* pancakes with greens and cheese, *buglama* meat stew, and *chigirtma*.[5] Whenever she wanted to say something, she prepared food.

I knew for sure that I inherited the shape of my lips from my mother since we both have full, clearly defined lips with a delicate pink color that my sister envied very much. Mama almost never used lipstick, other than for holidays and when we went to weddings. She never contradicted my father and she didn't answer him because she knew he didn't need her answer. The only people she spoke with were me, my sister,

---

4 *Shekarbura* is an Azerbaijani sweet (called şəkərbura in Azeri) of small yeasted hand pies with patterned designs on the outside and a filling of ground nuts, sugar, and cardamom.

5 *Chigirtma* is a dish made from chicken, eggplant, string beans, spinach, lamb, and eggs. In Azerbaijani, its name (çığırtma) means "scream." It's thought that the dish was named for the sounds the meat (or vegetables) make when being prepared in fiery hot fat.

and my *khala*;[6] my mother only berated my father behind firmly closed doors so he wouldn't hear. One time they completely stopped speaking and the only sound in the house was the television that my father regularly watched at full volume. Maybe that's why (or maybe that's because?) he never wanted to listen to anyone and lost his hearing over time until he could only hear with a hearing aid or if his conversation partner was very close. That was when Mama started speaking with him: as she prepared food she articulated everything she hadn't been able to say during thirty years of marriage.

She told us what we should wear, how to behave ourselves when visiting someone's home, and what we could and couldn't do, but she never used affectionate words. She generally gave out instructions and we knew, of course, that she loved us, despite never saying so out loud. Mama never valued words and was very surprised when she found out that I write poems: "Why do you devote yourself to such nonsense?" She periodically asked what I wrote about in them and always admonished that I not write too much. It worried her that I'm unable to keep quiet, that I always express and stand up for my point of view. I saw how she flinched when I opined out loud about things when male guests filled the house. My love of words was atypical: none of the women in my family liked words, though my maternal grandfather did. It was in his home that there were books, mostly atlases and medical reference volumes on subjects varying from

---

6 *Xaná*, or *khalá*, is an Azerbaijani word for an aunt who is one's mother's sister.

conjunctivitis to oncology, as well as books by Freud, Adler, and Jung. My grandfather knew Russian and dreamed of becoming a geographer.

Life, however, had other plans for him. He was a late child whose mother had long dreamed of having a son. And so seven sheep were slaughtered in the village when he was finally born. It was thanks to my grandfather's birth that his mother was able to remain married to her husband and give birth to three more boys: her husband had relentlessly left all the women who could not bear an heir for him. They so loved and watched over the boy that they decided to take him out of school early so he could study the land and how to care for it. He first grazed sheep, then cared for his sick brother, then for his parents . . . Until he met my grandmother.

She noticed him immediately because my grandfather was wearing dirty, stretched knit trousers and talking with the sheep surrounding him. She immediately realized he was as gentle and subtle as mountain flowers, that he would never forbid her to sew and would never limit her. And that's how it turned out: my grandfather never contradicted his wife when she was alive. It was as if he'd acquired a new parent after leaving the parental home since he did everything his wife ordered. His words were always as sweet as honey and he was the subtlest of his family line, the most fragile and the most malleable. If he noticed that my sister and I were longingly eyeing a box of candy, he'd take a couple pieces out for us when nobody was looking. All the sweets in the house were always stored in the least accessible place, atop a living room cabinet. My grandmother never opened candies or cookies received as gifts, instead hiding them up high and only taking them down when she expected guests.

My grandfather was the one who spoke with us: for him a river was a river, grass was grass, beautiful was beautiful, the sky was the sky, the earth was the earth. He never begrudged us his embraces and he gave us piggyback rides across mountain rivers even after we'd grown. The most important lessons that he gave: to love, to be affectionate and gentle, observe beauty, and choose our words carefully. We watched horror films together on a black-and-white television without sound, meaning we had to narrate the action ourselves, and we often watched movies in installments because the electricity was frequently shut off in the evenings. He loved telling stories and we could never determine if they were real or invented, so the world he had bequeathed to us ended when he died, falling into the river, just like his favorite white handkerchief once did. Green Georgian Tarkhun tarragon soda in a glass bottle, khachapuri in open village ovens, blue rivers, endless cornfields, spicy red beans on the table awaiting our arrival, and the mulberry and white cherry trees... Everything came together in a world of many colors, many flavors, many words—Tarkhun—khachapuri—river—corn—beans *gamarjoba*[7]—but all that died along with him. I couldn't speak when I learned of his death, nor sleep nor eat; he seemed everlasting, so I didn't believe he could die; he was as eternal as the mountains and the mulberry tree in the yard.

---

7 "Hello, hi" (Georgian).

I saw him last in a dream a few years ago. We were walking through a green field, a cemetery, but for some reason the gravestones were lying in the ground, as in a Catholic cemetery, rather than aiming skyward, as in a Muslim cemetery. He ordered me to count the stones, which I did, and then told him there were four. He asked me to count again. I quickly realized that those slabs were four pieces of his gravestone. The next morning I convinced my mother to call his wife (yes, he failed to keep his promise because he couldn't live in an empty house, so he married a second time, which he regretted right up until his own death) and ask her to check his grave. Lightning had hit his gravestone that night, evenly splitting it into four parts; that was his penultimate message. I received one more message just before my operation. I couldn't get to sleep for a long time and was lying in my bed, fingering my prayer beads. When I finally fell asleep, I found myself in the middle of an endless cornfield where my grandfather and I were walking together. He turned to me and said, "Everything will be fine, you'll still need to harvest corn for a long time."

I always spoke with him when things were the toughest, asking for help or advice. Even after dysarthria had distorted my speech, I knew he was still capable of catching what I said. Unlike others around me. Many people didn't even attempt to hear a sentence out to the end, rolling their eyes in annoyance as I overcame my own muscles and uttered another phrase. Without pills, my speech was like a rockslide, requiring tremendous effort from me and everyone around me. It was especially difficult to recite poetry: each line felt like a *saz*[8] string stretched to its limit. The words became tangible as if they were cold or warm, and I felt each word with my body, as each syllable cost my body effort. My voice was the first thing that changed after the operation—that's what everyone told me when I called them. My voice had become higher, softer, and more melodic; the hoarseness disappeared and my previous voice returned, though it no longer fit me. My voice seemed alien and unfamiliar, and it surprised me for several days. The stimulator sewn in under my right clavicle was similarly alien to me: I felt its foreignness, felt the wire along my neck, felt the stimulator's metal casing digging into my skin, and felt pain from the stitches on my head.

Sometimes I turn off the stimulator to see how things really are: the neurologist had immediately warned me that the stimulator is similar to a mask because it doesn't stop the illness; it only masks it. Without it I can no longer speak or close my mouth, which freezes up as if it were a death mask, open and eternally ready to scream.

---

8 A *saz* is a musical instrument similar to a lute. It is also known as a *baglama*.

V
SHOULDERS

When I was on my father's shoulders, the world seemed huge, filled with both horror and safety. On the one hand, I was scared because I had never climbed so high. On the other hand, I knew for certain that he wouldn't drop me. From my father's shoulders, the world seemed like a strange place: people moved around chaotically and seemed not to notice the uncharacteristically tall little girl. Trees raised their branches in surprise after realizing that someone had seen their bare trunks. This was a world resembling a huge aquarium containing creatures who could gobble me up but instead bumped against the glass, against my father's glassy shoulders. Coming of age deprived me of that feeling forever by changing my body so it no longer fit on my father's shoulders and, with time, was lowered to the ground, where being a body meant encountering other bodies.

My father loved repeating to me and my sister that we could feel at ease as long as he was alive: no one would ever harm us. Each time I went away for a scholarly conference or to work, he would call in the evening to ask if anyone had harmed me. The world, as my parents said, was not a safe place: anyone in it could harm (and certainly did cause pain to) others. If something happened at school or the university, my mother would mention that I needed to be more careful and cautious than others: I was not Russian, so I was necessarily an outsider, an other.

I first learned of my outsider status as a schoolgirl. My classmates pointed at me and hardly ever called me by name, often using rude terms instead. Sometimes their words transformed into gestures or actions: the most intolerant of my classmates once hit me as hard as he could with a basketball. My left index finger is swollen to this day, as a reminder that being a stranger means always having an enemy.

I have never forgotten my otherness since. I was an adolescent when Russian marches, skinhead attacks, and massive police raids at wholesale markets all began. Merchants and their employees at the markets were beaten every day and some of the victims died. My father's friend's son, who had flown to Russia for school vacation, left the house to refill his cellphone and was stomped to death by heavy boots.

My father worked at a wholesale market, so every evening was filled with apprehensive waiting: Would he return home today? Would someone harm him? If he was late, we started worrying and took turns rushing to call him on his cellphone.

The scariest incident of all happened one spring. My body will always remember that April. April 20, an ordinary sunny day, warm and pleasant. We were languishing in school, waiting for the bell since only one last lesson remained and we wanted to run outside as soon as possible, to have fun and eat candied fruit jellies from a nearby store. At some point, things got very noisy and the teacher's face crumpled like the quizzes we tossed in the wastebasket, to hide them from our parents' eyes. Our teacher was about to open her mouth to ask the class to be quiet, but then she realized the sound was outside, not inside. Everyone, even the teacher, rushed to look out the window. At first I thought a huge black beetle with lots of little limbs was crawling along the narrow street between the school and a shopping center, but when I looked closer I realized there were people. It was a crowd with black flags, a crowd of men, skinheads who were wearing heavy shoes and shouting. A bullhorn swallowed the syllables so I had to lean forward to hear. I convulsed in disgust when I caught their words; the tension in the classroom was palpable as my classmates went quiet, avoiding looking me in the eye. What came from the bullhorn was: *Russia for Russians*.

The bell rang and I waited for the crowd to disperse. But the people in black hadn't gone away, so my classmates and I decided to leave together, since the skinheads weren't likely to notice me among my classmates. We left the school and, as usual, I could barely drag the giant, horribly uncomfortable backpack that held all my books and notebooks. I wanted to get home as fast as possible, but somebody suggested going to the skate shop that sold cool backpacks, jackets, hats, and real skateboards. I wasn't interested in any of that and decided to wait for my classmates outside: it was hot and they promised to go in for only five minutes. I stood in front of the store and waited for them until I saw five skinhead men walking in my direction: one of them was holding a baseball bat and giving me a big smile. I immediately realized I had to run. One of my classmates saw what was happening through the window and ran out to get me. I don't remember who it was and I don't remember how long we ran; the only thing I remember is how much my shoulders ached from the heavy backpack, how the backpack hit my lower back, how I lost my breath, and how terrified I was. That was the first time I felt true primal danger and the proximity of death with my own skin. That was when I realized that being a stranger means being hated, being a vessel for rage.

I'd noticed that before, but had never reflected on how much people need a vessel for rage: an "other" is as necessary for those people as an empty beer can that can be kicked while walking or an old, scribbled sheet of paper that can be torn to shreds. Sometimes episodes of someone else's rage surface in my memory, like short films: there we were, my mother, my sister, and I, sitting in a tram on our way to run errands. Mama was still very young, with long black hair down to her chest, and she was wearing a dark blue blouse with shoulder pads and a knee-length skirt. My sister and I were talking about something in our children's language; I was six and my sister was four. When Mama asked us to hold the railings tightly, I met the gaze of an old woman sitting by the window.

I was six, but I knew for sure that rage and disgust filled her eyes. Animal carcasses tumbled out when she opened her mouth. She said that we *were overrunning things,* that *there was no work in this country because of us,* that we *were bringing our own into the world* (there was some bad word beginning with *v* after that) and that we *were living large.* I watched my mother, but my beautiful mother was keeping silent. She squeezed my shoulders hard and my shoulders slumped. She silently waited for our stop and I saw tears fill her eyes, though she didn't shed any. We got off the tram and she said: oh, *bala*[9], everyone is going to harm you.

We went to see Mama at work, where she was a nurse in the surgery department. When we walked in, someone addressed her as *Sveta*. Mama smiled and squeezed my shoulders hard when I asked why they were calling her someone else's name.

Every time I wanted to protect her and respond to an offender, she would lightly squeeze my shoulders, as if to remind me that we have no rights here, that we have no words, we cannot have any language, that we can't hit back at those who beat us because they're at home and it was an accident that we'd ended up as their cohabitants. My mother's shoulders always drooped—she tried to be pleasant and amenable to those around her so nobody would have any reason to insult her. Her shoulders bore every offensive word, every humiliation. All the words that were ever said to her had turned into

---
9 "Child" (Azerbaijani).

huge, dry stones. But she knew for certain that she wouldn't be humiliated or beaten up within the world of Turkish TV series. Words from TV characters filled her: she liked listening to endless dialogues delivered by Turkish actors and empathizing with them. The world viewed on a smartphone screen gave her a sense of safety, guaranteed she'd see beauty, and promised experiences that her reality so lacked.

My maternal grandmother's shoulders always drooped: her hands carried pails of water, sacks of beans and figs, and baskets for berries. Her shoulders drooped willingly. She knew her body was needed to feed and dress others, and she carried those dry stones on her shoulders until the end of her life.

I never saw my paternal grandmother's shoulders, but they probably drooped under the weight of her jealous husband's wrathful gaze so he could be sure that all her persistence had been forever transformed into a dry stone in his hand.

My shoulders, which drooped under my mother's hands, subsequently turned out to have been devoured by dystonia. One morning I suddenly realized that my right shoulder drooped unnaturally and there was no way I could return it to its normal position. The entire right side of my body was pulled to the ground as if magnetized. My back muscles, stomach muscles, shoulder muscles, and neck muscles reminded me of the feather stitch: they were impossible to untangle and they no longer belonged to me. I felt as if one of my hands would now stretch toward the ground forever, as if it belonged to a dervish, but the second hand lay limply on my body, no longer appealing to Allah.

After the operation, the first part of me that returned (after my voice) was my shoulders, which I strove to straighten each time I went somewhere or sat at a table. Two weeks after the stimulator was installed, I went to the neurosurgeon for an exam: he wavered for a long time but finally asked my permission to shut off the stimulator in order to make a "before" video. They filmed each patient before and after the operation, but for some reason mine hadn't been saved. I nodded and he confidently pressed a big red button on the remote. The right side of my body tightened in one second; my distorted neck hurt, my shoulders hurt, my back and abdominal muscles hurt, my foot turned to one side and hurt, my leg hurt after instantly becoming unbendable, almost metallic, my spasmodic arm hurt, and my speech broke into pieces that had trouble coming together. The doctor asked me to walk from one wall of the office to the other. As I dragged the right side of my body, attempting to think about something other than the pain and my regret that there weren't any handrails, he aimed the camera, striving to capture each anomalous movement. Then he set down the phone and switched on the stimulator. All of that took no more than a couple of minutes, but it felt as if an eternity had passed: it was surprising how quickly I'd adjusted to a normalized body and how rapidly I'd forgotten about pain, erasing every spasm from my head as if my body had always been capable of living without pain. I hungrily swallowed the opportunity not to know pain, thinking of other things and filling my head with sufferings and reflections beyond my own bodily shell. For the first month, I was afraid I'd wake up, that everything would turn out to be a dream or that my metal companion would break down. I listened suspiciously to any motion, scrutinized every muscle, and feared falling asleep.

Living free of physical pain meant seeing the world beyond the constraints of my own muscles and cells, listening to others, and recognizing their speech. Pain made me cranky and imprisoned me within my own skin; I was annoyed by the healthy bodies of others capable of speaking, breathing, and moving effortlessly. My girlfriends annoyed me by joyfully discussing future plans and new partners, and whenever I got together with women I knew from high school I cried for a long time on the way home, out of fury and injustice. I saw no future because my eyes could only see pain and another dead end for my body as it succumbed to slow disintegration. I felt like I was turning into a statue, ossifying from within and becoming desiccated stone, a vessel for fury.

My father's large shoulders didn't protect me from pain. They had taken into account everything but my body. I acquired a body when I was born and now my existence depended only on those muscles, cells, tissues, and the circulatory and central nervous systems, as well as on the vegetative nervous system, hormones, and whatever would happen to my body if, say, it were to fall, experience trauma, get sick, catch germs, or be attacked by viruses. Metal forceps greeted my body when I was born, leaving two hollows in my head. After my head was shaved, I was surprised to find four old scars: who, exactly, did what to my body still remained partially unexplained but, unlike memory, the body never lies. My body stores facts with surprising precision: it doesn't misrepresent them, instead remembering forever what happened to it, meaning that I have archival scars, scratches, bruises, or burn marks here and there. My body forgives no misdeeds. The only thing it can easily forget is pain.

VI

HANDS

The most important parts of a woman's body were her hands: they prepared food, rocked children, did laundry, ironed men's shirts, sewed clothes, swept, washed the floor, and dusted. A woman's hands were always supposed to be busy—only a man's hands were entitled to be carefree. While men's hands lay idly on a set table, women's hands carried dishes of food, arranged plates, rolled dough to be cut into squares for *khangayal*, stuffed grape leaves, served platters of plov, and hemmed wedding dresses. Any woman in our family knew that her hands were not given to her for writing.

My maternal grandmother's wrinkled hands moved quickly and easily, and they'd always been accustomed to work; the skin on the back of her hands resembled singed paper. Her agile hands noticed every loose thread on a dress and immediately concealed it from the back of the fabric. They tightened loose buttons that were ready to fall off. If her hands happened to be near a tree, they'd pick a whole basket of mulberries and figs in no time. Her hands knew that Allah would transform any task they performed into a day in Paradise.

My paternal grandmother's hands also knew no rest: they prepared food for four children, tidied the home, gardened, ran their fingers over fabric, lugged water, rolled thin dough for *kutaby* pancakes, rinsed rice for plov, and picked over raisins, but they never wrote anything. Tasks were her words. The flawlessly decorated home displayed itself to unexpected guests as if it were a rare manuscript: objects, each in its own place, recalled commas and semicolons that had cautiously hidden themselves within the body of a sentence.

My mother's hands were always at work, too, and our hands were similar: long, slender fingers with large oval nails. My mother's hands were almost always in water, washing dishes, washing windows, washing the floor. They tirelessly bathed the world around her, as if only that cleansing could make it more pleasant. It was my mother who taught my sister and me about cleanliness, though this was not an ordinary cleanliness but a persnickety, almost neurotic cleanliness. If she noticed a spot on a mug that had just been washed, it needed to be rewashed; dirty dishes had to be washed immediately after a meal; and the floor was scrubbed so every corner sparkled. Even the light switches were sanitized with alcohol wipes. Cleanliness calmed my mother, giving her a sense of control, as if she were capable of managing her own life after all. The home was her true domain: jars, bottles, spices, and grains were the little things she herself could select, and she even spent hours choosing a hook for the bathroom. Of course IKEA was her favorite store: Mama wandered for hours through the ideal Scandinavian interiors, running her fingers over dishes, examining hooks, pondering domestic utensils. This was her way of meditating. Even choosing a pillowcase took forever. First she would quickly glance at all the pillowcases displayed in the store, then she'd recall our linens, reflect on what color would fit best in the dark-brown bedroom, read about the fiber content, and choose the fabric while also, of course, comparing the size of the pillowcase with the size of the pillow before finally choosing the item she considered worthy.

The women I knew treated the interiors of their apartments more seriously than their own faces or health. They were always tense when hosting guests because they knew this was a competition of sorts, that their apartments would certainly be evaluated: every little corner, from floor to ceiling, from the tiles in the bathroom to the balcony, from the type of laminate on the floor to the wallpaper in the children's room. Everything was discussed and each detail was subjected to criticism because homes were the sole form of self-expression. It was easy to determine who lived better than the rest since they aimed to accentuate their own prosperity rather than hide it. They bought monstrous furniture with gilded detailing, crammed beautifully arrayed dishes into cupboards, sewed expensive fabrics into heavy drapes, usually valances with side panels. There wasn't one iota of truth in those homes because they were furnished like museums and curated with the viewer in mind, and every sign of real life in the inhabitants' rooms was banished, hidden away in bedside tables and desk drawers. Homes were women's small islands. In the depths of the hostess's living room, the women could let their hands rest for a short while, holding only a Turkish tea glass and sipping tea with bergamot and thyme. Those hands were occasionally embellished by a manicure and smoothed with hand cream before, for example, a wedding. My mother never polished her nails without a reason, but if a celebration lay ahead, she made an appointment with a manicurist friend and gladly went to have her nails done. This was a cherished occasion: rare hours when she could spend money on her own body without twinges of guilt. For a few days she would gaze at her painted nails with enchantment, as if she were a child who had finally received a much-desired toy.

But my mother never took off her ring. Other women in our family circle also never took off their rings, which signified marriage and belonging to a specific man; they wore gold wedding rings with precious gemstones. Jewelry accompanied unmarried young women along the path to entering womanhood. Hands that weren't busy with anyone or anything resembled a blank sheet of paper: an initial first sentence appeared and was then followed by a long text that they hoped would continue for a lifetime. Putting a ring on an unknowing young woman's hand for the first time during an engagement is a symbol of constraint and an impending wedding.

The future husband's relatives should not skimp on earrings, bracelets, and other gold jewelry since they, after all, need to show the bride's family that they're prepared not only to take her into their circle but also provide for all her needs. An engagement was almost always followed by marriage: my cousins proudly displayed the rings on their hands, joyfully counting the days until the wedding with joyful anticipation. The presence of a ring meant they had fulfilled their primary daughterly duty, so they strove to tell everyone around them about it. The engagement was followed by *khna-yakhty*,[10] when the bride-to-be wears a red dress symbolizing her innocence as she parts with her previous life; her pure hands are covered in henna, painted with promise. Never again will her hands be empty; a child will follow the ring, and a second child will follow the first. A woman's hands should not be empty and they should not write—that is the first rule that a young woman learns, even before entering into marriage.

Hands were allowed to dance at weddings, performing gentle flowing motions that resembled ocean waves, in exchange for banknotes that were placed in them. The more alluringly a woman's hands danced, the more attention and money those hands received. But these dances did not tell stories: their goal wasn't to attract a man but to express joy at someone else's happiness, to offer praise to great Allah, who gave this young man to this young woman. Mature women were masters of their hands, controlling each muscle and

---

10 *Khna-yakhty* is a transliteration of the Russian хна-яхты, which is in turn a transliteration of the Azeri *xınayaxdı*. In this ceremony, the bride parts with her father's home and her innocence the night before the wedding, and her hands are decorated with henna patterns. The first letter of the groom's name is written on one palm, the first letter of the bride's on the other.

each finger as they turned their palms away from and toward themselves at just the right time, twirling as if they were stuffing grape leaves.

All the women in our family wanted more than anything to hold children in their hands: their hands yearned when they weren't lulling a child to sleep, when they weren't rocking a child's fragile body under the unwavering gaze of the moon.

After my brother was born, my mother lulled him to sleep, carrying him around the apartment. Children were her main consolation and they made life extraordinary. Her hands had missed the sweet feeling of fullness. The arrival of children into the world brought events, served as the basis for conversation, and became a source of pride, but children always grew up and no longer fit in her hands. Children became more than their own childish bodies and stopped needing a mother, which was what distressed her most of all. Once children had grown up, they removed not only themselves but also the need to cook, do laundry, and wash floors. The days became empty and monotonous, and she got their news by telephone or in a conversation, as a chance witness, since feelings and events were no longer a part of her. It was when she stopped being a participant in the lives of her own children that her hands began to yearn.

Her hands never wrote, but they sought work. So during a particularly lonely year she got the idea of renovating the apartment: she scraped and varnished the doors herself, painted chairs, and decorated a space that she was sure would never abandon her.

I knew that a man's hands seldom cooked; my father basically just skewered meat and grilled kebabs. Money was also only in my father's masculine hands: he gave us small amounts of pocket money and gave my mother money for buying furniture or appliances. In my father's opinion, that was how a family man should behave: earn money, bring it home, and distribute it so it can later be exchanged for groceries or material items. Every morning after another scene, after an episode of jealousy and rage, after my father had beaten my mother, he would come home with a bag full of groceries and hold it out to us. My father would buy what my sister and I loved most of all: Tempo chocolates, pineapples, candied fruit jellies, and chewing gum. It was as if he was trying to buy our silence, to exchange my mother's bruises for candy. Scariest of all was that we couldn't refuse since he knew what we loved and knew that chocolate could buy two little girls' hearts. These were poisoned sweets, saturated with a simple and obvious family law: men's hands are allowed to lash out, to control the entire home, keeping everything in check. He exchanged the millimeters and centimeters of my mother's beaten body for candy: the harder he'd beaten her the night before, the more candy was offered to us, and the scarier the temptation for me and my sister. He trained us in silence, in obedience, and nobody dared stop his hands when he opened another bottle of vodka to pour himself a glass.

My father often lamented that we'd become so Russian, that we'd lost our language, forgotten our traditions, and resembled our Russian girlfriends, saying that if he'd taken us away early enough, we would have grown up like normal children. But he became Russian fastest of all. He let bitter Russian vodka enter his blood and could no longer live without it. When we were still very little, my father dreamed of the day he'd return to his native land, his motherland, but it was vodka that managed to drown his southern body in its own hot water. The older we grew, the more regretful and disillusioned he became and the more vodka he drank in the evenings. My mother tired of putting up with my father's drunken escapades and finally decided to have him treated. One of her friends suggested a healer in our region. Nobody knew exactly what he did with his patients but one thing was certain: they stopped drinking. The healer led my father into his office and firmly closed the door. Twenty or thirty minutes later he came out and said my father wouldn't drink for six years. Whether that was by chance or intention, my father did not drink for exactly six years.

He was better without alcohol. He became gentle and affectionate, tended toward chattiness, and joked like a child. All the best about him, everything that I truly loved, had returned. When Papa didn't drink, he seemed to be a good person: generous, open, and possibly naïve. He loved talking with a variety of people and was always genuinely interested in how things were for saleswomen in stores; he brought home all the stray dogs and cats in the area; and he adored cartoons and cried when he watched *Wait for Me*. I couldn't figure out how it was that these two people lived inside him: the tender and naïve Papa who was happy to see marmosets at the zoo with us, and the other one, a man I didn't know, who would harshly fling my mother to the floor because she was late coming home from work. I liked it most of all when he smiled, but I still feared I'd be hit and flinched whenever he held out his hands to hug me. I knew too well what his hands were capable of since I knew their strength and their mercilessness.

When we were in high school, my sister and I managed to convince our father to buy a dog. My father insisted on a purebred, typical because he liked choosing what was flashy, expensive, and noticeable: those things reinforced his sense of self-worth and allowed him to show off to his friends. At the pet market, my father almost convinced us to buy a dog bred for fighting, but those fancy white dogs with long muzzles were very expensive and not at all attractive. Then we suddenly noticed a little black creature peering out of a box. A German shepherd, the last puppy in the litter. The vendor was so glad for our interest that she sold him to us for next to nothing. We later realized that ill health was the reason the price was so low: he was sluggish, sleepy, and refused to eat. The vet prescribed injections that had to be administered every day and, yes, only my father could bring himself to stick the needle into the dog. Only my father could inflict pain on creatures he loved. When the dog was larger, he ultimately (to my mother's joy) needed to be given to a family friend because they had their own house and we didn't have much space in our apartment. This was the first time in my life that I parted with a beloved creature: my sister and I hugged the black puppy for a long time as he licked our hands, suspecting nothing. It's unclear if he remembers that betrayal, but he recognized us even a couple of years later, cheerfully putting his paws on our shoulders and licking our faces.

My hands knew how to wash and cook, but they liked writing more than anything. They always liked writing, which is why even in my childhood I had notebooks where I wrote stories and thought up characters, even attempting to draw them. Writing gave me conversation partners I could talk with at any time, writing didn't depend on anyone but me, and writing was always with me, like an invisible amulet. If someone wronged and upset me, I'd wait until evening to open my notebook and write a story where something bad happens to a bad character and something good happens to the good character. Only later did it become obvious to me that this is not always how things are: bad things happen to good characters, too, and life adds all kinds of people into its soup, tossing in spices without asking who likes what.

After my hands started shaking, it was as if there were tiny, barely perceptible earthquakes in them that nobody else could notice. The doctor wrote the word *tremor* in my records and convinced me it would pass. But the more time went by, the more my hands didn't respond to me: they might twitch at inopportune moments and my fingers periodically writhed spasmodically, but the most painful cramps were around my elbows, as if someone invisible were attempting to pull one of the bones. Dystonia eventually took my hands, too. The muscles in my shoulders and forearms cramped up and stiffened, as if cement had been poured into them; I was periodically unable to bend my arms at the elbow or unclench my fingers.

My right hand particularly suffered, as did the entire right side of my body. Was there some symbolism in the fact that it was the righteous, "pure" side that was now diminished? As a child, I wrote with my left hand, but my mother insisted that I be retaught since writing left-handed was considered incorrect, something in which religion may have played a role, too; in Islam the entire left side of the body is considered impure, which is why on the Day of Judgment sinners receive their book of deeds in their left hand. As a result, I began writing with my right hand, diligently tracing out large, correct letters nestling affectionately against one another. I wrote with my right hand until it refused to serve me.

VII
TONGUE

EVERYBODY AT SCHOOL SPOKE RUSSIAN, but at home I heard Azeri and Turkish in the television series that Mama watched. It was obvious to me as a child that if I spoke several languages there would be several different versions of me. I was Russian in the big world of school or in the yard, but I was Azerbaijani in the small world of family.

There were also specific words that were never translated, that seemed to simply exist like plants and flowers: those words were what they were, existing organically and inexplicably like parts of the body, like secret knowledge without which it would be impossible to fathom the family history. My ancestors' words burned like hot coals inside my mouth and my voice box, leaving scorch marks. And so when my mother poured boiling water from a pot, she inevitably uttered, "*Bismillah ir-Rahman ir-Rahim.*"[11] And if someone was going away for a long time, she had to spill some water after they left and say, "*yol açık olsun,*"[12] and if we were far away and

---

11 "In the name of God, the compassionate, the merciful" (Arabic). This phrase opens every sura of the Koran except the ninth.

12 "Have a good trip, may the road be open" (Azerbaijani).

my mother was worrying a lot, she finished the conversation with the phrase "*Allah'a emanet ol.*"[13] Each appeal referred to an age-old ancestral agreement, *qurban olum*, meaning "may I sacrifice myself for you." At one time the tribe decided that love entailed the capacity for self-sacrifice, so its members determined that forgoing one's own body guaranteed the prosperity of the community. It also decided that only a knife plunged into flesh attests to love. These phrases were unrelated to human love and were instead needed to demonstrate one's love for Allah, the Merciful and Compassionate.

Going to visit my father's relatives in Baku meant I would need to speak only one language, something that became harder with every passing year. The relatives often mocked our accents, and Russian words had forced out Azerbaijani equivalents over time. I noticed that most people knew Russian and that some had graduated from Azerbaijani high schools, where they were taught in Russian and were referred to as being in the "Russian sector," and I sometimes felt as if we hadn't left Russia at all. My tongue had difficulty switching to Turkish articulation because speaking Russian was significantly easier. The language confidently emerged from my mouth, which produced choppy, resonant, loud, and sharp sounds resembling those of a butcher's cleaver, though that same knife had, of course, cut off my second tongue. The language of my mother and father, the language of my maternal and paternal grandmothers, is soft and flowing, a language where one

---

[13] "Trust in Allah" (Azerbaijani).

sound smoothly transitions into another, a language that is as fast-moving and agile as Azerbaijani mountain streams, a language that eluded me in the thick white fog of Gabala.[14] I lost my language gradually, as if it were an organ that slowly failed me and initially felt restorable, as if I would always be able to return to it, switching it back on again whenever I needed it. But as time went on I had fewer and fewer Azerbaijani words: the organ had stopped fulfilling its function and lay powerless in my mouth. My parents were afraid that if they didn't speak with us in Russian we wouldn't be able to learn the language and study, so we most often heard Russian at home; books in Russian later began appearing there, too.

Russian books first came into my life at the children's library not far from home, where I went as regularly as if to a job, meaning the librarians recognized me and affectionately set aside new arrivals. I loved wandering around the various sections and gathering up all kinds of books: I recall being engrossed in reading the Japanese writer Masahiko Shimada, scrutinizing a Dale Carnegie book, and reading Spanish detective novels. All those books were in Russian, which became an intermediary between me and the world of literature. I felt as if books were acceptable djinns: they took over the consciousness and twisted time into a slender straw, telling stories about people who resembled me a lot or not at all, telling of love and devotion, of death and dying. They were portable sanctuaries that conversed with me. I always took a few hefty books along

---

14 Gabala, which is also known as Qabala in English (Qəbələ in Azerbaijani, and Габала in Russian) is a town in northern Azerbaijan.

when we set off to visit my father's relatives in Baku or see my mother's relatives in a small Georgian village. Books helped me hide from my feelings of shame over my horrible pronunciation and ridiculous accent, forgotten phrases and everyday expressions, and my wayward and strange desires. My face was solidly hidden behind books in all the family photographs, which may be why Bibi called me "the Russian professor." I felt something break inside me every time the relatives made fun of me and my sister at family meals and affectionately called us *rus bala*.[15] I didn't understand why they considered us Russian children. We were, after all, reminded of the opposite every day in Russia, told that we weren't Russian children, which was specifically what rankled our classmates and those around us. We were outsiders. Where, then, was our home if we didn't belong here, either? Were we not seen as part of the world? It turned out that we didn't fit into either of the worlds, like defective puzzle pieces. What happens to puzzle pieces that don't fit no matter which way you turn them? Is there a place for pieces like that? And where, in that case, is the "motherland"? Or maybe we really had become *rus bala*, given that we read and wrote in Russian? How had it happened that the only language I could express myself in found no affectionate ways to address me, instead flinging insults at me like lifeless kernels of corn, reminding me that I'm black, blackie, black-ass, alien, monster, foreigner, foreign-born, and extraneous? I'd become part of that language, but it was poisoning me like contaminated water, and the words burned

---

[15] "Russian child" (Azerbaijani).

like the bodies of plague victims, piercing my alien body, my Eastern woman's body, my Eastern woman's sickly, thickening body. How was I to speak of that body?

Although we were also considered "strangers" in Baku, the rule of "malicious tongues" still applied to us. Those around us didn't just have malicious eyes; they had malicious tongues, too, and of course that's considered more dangerous. Venomous tongues were never silent: the eye was incapable of conveying someone else's shame but the tongue, by contrast, broke what had been seen into tiny pieces and then transformed those pieces into sentences, passing them on from one person to another, slowly poisoning everything around them. Everyone knew there was nothing worse than becoming the subject of gossip. In the world I grew up in, you existed as long as people talked about you: if they spoke well of you, your parents and relatives were glad because that meant worthy parents had created a worthy person. If people spoke poorly of you, though, their faces clouded over since you weren't a beloved child. You had instead been turned into a red mark of shame, the thick tar of disappointment, and there was nothing worse than bringing shame upon your parents.

In order not to become a victim of malicious tongues, one often needed to keep quiet and do little because deeds, akin to djinns, were invisible yet tangible. And, like ghouls who devoured the bodies of the dead, the local women transformed the stories of travelers into a feast of dishy gossip about misdeeds.

A man's actions were considered the appetizer since they were, after all, *men*, and were thus allowed to make mistakes, beat their wives, cheat on them, and have second families. It was as if their very birth, the possibility of continuing the family line, and passing on a name compensated for their future wrongdoing.

The soup course—the women's deeds—followed. It was a stew of scrutiny, discerning which housewife was insufficiently hospitable, whose food didn't stand up to criticism, who had been stingy on her children's weddings and skimped on meat, and whose dress had turned out to be immodest. Women were supposed to be irreproachably righteous and everything they did interested everyone: just one improperly uttered word, a dress that was too short, or a photo with a glass of wine posted on social media meant you could say goodbye to that wedding dress forever. This was why all my female cousins never posted anything of substance online: the social media pages they did set up were entirely impersonal, adorned with flowers or distant landscapes rather than portraits. Their timelines looked like collections of recipes and beauty tips. None of them ever wrote much about anything since that would have meant compromising themselves and being served up at the djinns' feast.

Finally, the children's misdeeds were offered as the main dish. They were discussed longer than anything else: who had tied the knot and who was single, who had divorced and why, who had children, who still didn't have children and why, who worked and where, who earned how much money, and who was shaming the family. The worst sinners were discussed the longest and the marrow was sucked from their bones like a healing elixir. Once sated, the guests were like *ifrits*[16], filling a room's emptiness with their nasty, rough tongues, which grew larger than their bodies, occupying the entire space and touching anyone who happened to peer inside.

My mother's tongue was sadness: it could be spoken in Russian, Azerbaijani, or Turkish, but it was invariably sad and it always had words for prayers, entreaties, and suras, though a sense of yearning was most important. A yearning for the life she'd left behind forever, as if a photograph from thirty years ago, just after she'd turned eighteen, was eternally staring at her: she'd cut her unflattering bangs and dreamed of becoming a model. Eighteen-year-old Mama is looking into the camera defiantly, anticipating that strange and rather complicated life. She doesn't yet know my father will choose her and that she, believing in true love, will elope with him, despite her parents' interdictions. She won't become a model, nor will she go to medical school since the entry exam for chemistry that year will be replaced with an exam for physics, which she doesn't know well, and she doesn't know that an application to the medical college is only for nursing. She also doesn't know that a dorm room will be turned into a privatized apartment where she'll be living when she has her two daughters and one son. She doesn't know that she'll never

---

16 *Ifrits* are a demonic type of djinn with many powers; they appear in Muslim and Arabic mythology.

return to her parents' home in the middle of a Georgian field, where first her mother and then her father died. She doesn't know that her childhood home will pass into the hands of her father's second wife, a treacherous, indiscreet, and greedy woman who endlessly asked for money. A woman who would cut all the trees in their garden down to the roots, even the big mulberry tree whose branches the children had loved to lie on. There was always a sense of heartache in my mother's speech, as if this heartache were a stone at the very bottom of each of her sentences, though this was not simply heartache—it was heartache filled with doubt: *What if I had done things differently?*

She never asked my father that question. Women generally never spoke directly with men—even with a father or brother, since conversation was filtered through a fine screen that held back the most important, large, brave, lavish, and truthful words. Fathers and husbands never knew the full story of their own wives' and children's lives because the men saw them only at family celebrations, in photos, and on short trips, meaning that wives and children for them were little images that lacked words. That's why I knew that my father strongly disliked both my ability to choose my words and my big mouth, which was capable of shouting, revealing djinns, and saying the unspeakable. Even back when I was a little girl, it embarrassed him that I was constantly asking questions. His wariness increased as I grew up and he kept wondering who would want to marry a woman who talked endlessly. When the dysarthria hit, my words ran out and transformed into boulders trapped in my voice box: I forced out each word like Sisyphus pushing the boulder, attempting to turn it into sound. At some point, spoken and written words took on differing weights: it was easier for me to write something down than to say it, and when I completely stopped speaking, I started to write, violating the first commandment of women in our family.

Dysarthria didn't just affect my articulation. It also changed my voice, which became coarse and low, as if my throat was forcing it out instead of my diaphragm; my speech had become as slow and choppy as Morse code. I periodically felt I was losing control of my tongue, and it was especially awkward to sit in the dentist's chair and discover that no matter how I tried not to prevent him from doing his work, my tongue's movements were insidious and willful, reminding me of two things: my own helplessness and how the tongue is a muscle not unlike a pagan dancing around a campfire.

I stopped singing because of the illness and even felt relieved to have already quit opera singing. Music became one of my languages when I was a schoolgirl: it was a secret and personal language, a language for conversing more with the dead than with the living. I liked singing more than speaking because music lent new meanings to words, dressing them in new clothes. Singing also meant adding beauty to meaning and immortalizing words. I first learned I could sing when our music teacher announced tryouts for a school chorus. She accepted me right away because she was struck by my vocal range and wrote the unfamiliar word *soprano* next to my name. My parents didn't like idle talk, so they didn't like idle singing either. That meant I had to lie. One day I said I'd be home late because of an after-school activity, another day I was doing homework with classmates, then there was the time I went to the bookstore... I kept thinking up all kinds of new excuses so I'd be able to go to rehearsals. In a world where life is strictly regimented, lying is a necessary protective measure, akin to a life preserver at the public pool. But the language of singing worked differently from all the other languages I'd previously known. You couldn't tell lies or be deceptive while singing; you just had to know the twelve notes, learn to breathe with your diaphragm, and open your mouth properly while also weaving your own suffering into each sound. There is nothing more intimate and fascinating than singing a melody along with strangers: by listening carefully, you'll easily discover that everyone is singing about something slightly different. One's currently in love, another's worried about problems with their parents, and somebody else is thinking about the future, so each individual note takes on a new shade.

I liked spending time in the big music classroom next to the teacher's black grand piano. We watched a Queen concert, often sang duets (alto and soprano), sang Ukrainian lullabies from her childhood, and listened to Beethoven. Despite our age difference, at some point we went from being teacher and student to becoming friends: she shared her feelings about divorce, mourned her ex-husband, who had died from a sudden aneurism, and brought in her grandson and daughter. On the very worst days, we simply sat next to each other and sang duets. Given my vocal characteristics and range of octaves, she thought it would be worth my while to continue singing and pursue a career in opera. We went for an audition with a producer, who put me in front of a big microphone, gave me earphones, and asked me to sing some samples. That was an unfamiliar feeling for me, as if I were singing into a void or a black hole: the sound that came out of my mouth burned up instantly in the space around me, like a cigarette butt tossed from overhead. The producer agreed with the teacher and gave me a week to think about it. If I decided to sing, he'd help me continue learning. I lay in my room and thought about which of the two forbidden things I loved more—singing or writing—and though my voice resembled a Japanese camellia bud and I didn't yet have dysarthria, something inside me was indistinctly signaling *write*. Writing was more complex, hence more interesting, and writing meant tearing at my skin, tearing out pieces of my own body with no painkillers at all so those pieces could populate others' imaginations. And so I decided to turn down singing. A few years later I discovered that was my wisest decision because dystonia destroyed my soprano voice and turned me into an alto, taking away yet another of my joys and burying it under a heap of dry stones.

VIII
BACK

My grandfather often kissed me on the back, right on a beauty mark between my shoulder blades. He said that was "the prophet's seal," that only sainted people could have that sort of beauty mark and that the prophet Muhammad (may Allah bless him and grant him peace) had that same sort of beauty mark (more specifically a birthmark). And although my mother insisted repeatedly that I have it removed—it was too big and very unfavorably located—I left it as a reminder of my grandfather.

Nobody else in our family had beauty marks on their back, and for some unknown reason I was the only one who received a large brown one between the shoulder blades. It seemed more likely to me that it was a "grandfather's seal" rather than "the prophet's seal" since my grandfather left not only his kiss but also the best of himself on that mark. He conveyed the most important things of all to me with that kiss: love is the ability to read others' bodies, to see the good in the mundane, and to see light in darkness.

He often carried my sister and me piggyback. We'd climb up on his big, broad back, embrace his neck, and observe as he showed us mountain streams and cornfields, and told of plants and village buildings. He lugged us around even when we were too heavy for him, managing to overcome shortness of breath and episodes of nausea.

In addition to children, he hauled large sacks with corn, beans, figs, and black coal. He worked as a stoker in his final years: each day he had to toss coal into a stove, blow on it, monitor the pressure, and clean the boiler and damper. Try as he might to wash his hands clean, there were still traces of black coal underneath his fingernails and he himself was covered in fine dust from head to toe; poisonous fumes slowly saturated his lungs. At first, my grandfather had bad dizzy spells and felt hot, but over time his body seemed to grow used to the black veil of heat and dust, and the dizziness passed. The only thing that upset him was the need to wash himself before hugging children, lest they be covered in dust, too, and spread it through the house. His wife would boil three buckets of water, pour the hot water into a big metal bathtub, adding a fourth bucket of cold water from the well, then leave him with the basins and buckets, and herd the children away. My grandfather always had to wash by the light of a ceramic lamp that gave off a harsh smell and simultaneously made you feel a little nauseous and sleepy. He would take a small piece of soap and start methodically scrubbing every part of his body, especially his hands and face. Since the blackness had seeped into him, it didn't all wash off: it had become part of him, an extension, just as his children and his wife were an extension of him. Despite his dirty and difficult work, he'd smile dreamily when he opened a bottle of fizzy Tarkhun tarragon water before going to bed and say the time would come when we could go travel the world and draw our own map.

He was never able to draw his own map. The black coal destroyed his body, methodical and unnoticed: nobody paid any attention initially to a goiter that appeared, but it grew larger and larger with each year, as if it were attempting to burst out from underneath his thin skin. The local doctor had never seen the likes of it and suggested it was simply inflammation from the dust. When an oncologist finally examined my grandfather, it turned out that a malignant tumor had already managed to metastasize in all his organs. There were tumors everywhere—in his lungs, kidneys, and lymph nodes—though that didn't force him to quit smoking. Standing in the yard for a while with a cigarette was his favorite thing to do because time needed no purpose when he smoked. Time simply flowed, along with the smoke issuing from his mouth.

My father's father loved smoking, too, and even died with a smoldering cigarette in his hand while sitting across from a portrait of his wife. He carried on his back the heavy burden of pathological jealousy that had been passed down to him by his own father, my great-grandfather. He was jealous of anyone who came near his wife. He perceived as her potential lover anyone—a guest in his home, the neighbors, the mail carrier—whose gaze lingered upon her, if only briefly. Years passed and his rage strengthened like fine cognac and hardened like the bark of an old tree until that rage became an organic part of him: no longer could any of the village residents recall him without a scowl and knitted black brows. He considered a bruise on his wife's knee, which she got falling down the stairs, to be the consequence of a tryst. The fact that his wife hardly ever left the house didn't calm him since my father's father was convinced both of his wife's infidelity and that all praise is for Allah—Lord of all worlds, the most Compassionate, Most Merciful, Master of the Day of Judgment. He passed the stone of burning jealousy down to his younger son, my father.

My father only discovered that stealthy inheritance the moment he met his future wife, my mother. When he saw her brown eyes observing a bride and groom from beneath her brows, my father immediately realized that those eyes should now look only at him. He didn't like school and he didn't get into the university because of his poor Russian, and all that interested him about vocational school was the opportunity to talk with others. And so when his best friend suggested that my father open a wholesale outlet, my father didn't have to think for long. He acted quickly since he needed money but had no job. The two of them chipped in to rent a metal storage container at a market. Over the years he sold pitchforks, shovels, shovel shafts, and chains. He lugged heavy boxes on his back for days at a time, first from the supplier to the store, then from the store to the client. After all that, the goods he laid outside for the workday were brought inside for the night and set out again in the morning. His back hurt more and more with each year until he eventually had to hire a loader. He started drinking to relieve the pain: first a couple of shots, then a few, and finally a whole glass of vodka. He felt sorry for himself because he'd never wanted that sort of life. His hands weren't aspiring to pointlessly move pieces of metal around: they wanted to till a garden in his native Zangilan, plant olive trees, pet dogs and cats, plaster the walls of his father's house, turn the wheel of a tractor trailer truck, and drive around to cities and villages.

Over time, the dry stone of caustic jealousy joined the pain on his back: he went to the hospital to see his wife at work and beat up the gynecological surgeon she regularly worked with, scowled at neighbors on our landing, and stopped inviting friends over for food and drinks. My father thought all men were attempting to possess his wife. Since he didn't trust her, he checked messages and calls on her cellphone, never let her go out alone or without the children, then finally forbade her to work, so she would not be in the company of men. She didn't work for twenty whole years, instead sitting with her children and thinking he'd calm down, that her fading beauty and lost youth would bring him to his senses. But the years passed and his rage strengthened like fine cognac and settled into him as if it were the roots of an old tree, becoming an organic part of him, so that nobody remembered him without the scowl and knitted black brows. After losing his hearing, he became even more mistrustful and heard male voices when his wife was taking a shower. My father would burst into the bathroom, filled with ripened rage and seeing red as he searched for the lover; he also periodically guarded the front door, certain that his wife's lovers would arrive as soon as he left the apartment. He was akin to a madman, though while Majnun[17] had detected his own madness and hidden in the desert, my father darted around the apartment like an exhausted bull. We feared him in those moments and were more afraid of him than anything on Earth: he didn't hear anyone and his eyes darted from side to side, as if he were watching a black-and-white film that only he could see.

All the women in the house went silent and we shut ourselves in a room, listening closely, wondering if the beast had fallen asleep. Once he was sleeping, everyone left the room to take food out of the kitchen, pour some water, and gather the broken dishes off the floor. We tiptoed around, trying not to make any noise, knowing that when he was enraged he no longer distinguished us from others: to him, every woman seemed to be a creature deserving of rage. Nothing calmed us like the sound of the front door closing since it meant he had gone. The absence of sound meant he was sleeping. We hated our father after those scenes; we hated his harsh hands, threatening back, scary head whirling with persistent thoughts, hated the paternal genes we'd received and the parts of our bodies we'd inherited from him. Once he cooled down, he'd try to pretend nothing had happened and become deliberately affectionate and generous, throwing money

---

17 Majnun is a madman possessed by a djinn in an Arab story. The main character of Nizami Ganjavi's poem *Layla and Majnun* loses his mind and goes into the desert after the father of his beloved fellow tribeswoman Layla gives her in marriage to another man.

around, buying groceries and our favorite sweets, apparently hoping that food would force us to forget his cruelty and that the sweetness of chocolate would drown out the bitter taste of his rage. He was angry that we supported Mama, that we always took her side, so our mutual grievances angered him, too: if Mama didn't speak with him, neither did we.

It was like that in all the families I knew: responsibility for a daughter's behavior fell on maternal shoulders, so if a daughter made a mistake it was the mother who paid because it was her responsibility, after all, to raise the worthy parents' worthy daughter. If we did something our father didn't like, that inevitably meant our mother would also suffer the punishment since she was the one raising bad daughters. The collective responsibility we felt for one another motivated us to behave warily so his rage wouldn't descend on all of us like an avalanche. That had a reverse effect, though: by inflicting pain on our mother, our father inflicted pain on us, too, drowning us in her tears so scars remained not only on her exhausted body but also in our memories, destroying his good deeds as quickly as he destroyed kitchenware.

On my mother's back, on my maternal grandmother's back, and on my paternal grandmother's back—on any woman's back—one can see the bond connecting a mother to a daughter, and a daughter to a sister. If one chose her words, another answered for them, which may be why at some point they all stopped speaking, stopped opening their mouths, and stopped writing and uttering words.

As Mama aged, her back began aching frequently: the hours spent washing floors, windows, stove burners, the bathroom, and the tiles had made themselves known, returning to her as pain, though she never complained since anyway, how could that pain be compared to the pain from my father's blows? She'd grown used to it over the course of violent years, just as I was used to spasms, and she'd begun thinking that a pained body is a normal body, and that minor pain is just a reminder that we're still alive. She knew that all women had to live with pain and husbands beat all of them except her mother, who was a rare exception to the rule. In her youth, Mama still attempted to resist and the police came to the house a couple of times, but they let my father go, saying that these were family matters. On rare days when other women were in the house, they'd sit down at the table and share stories, nearly whispering, and one of them would periodically dare admit something awful, like a husband's infidelity or beatings. The women exchanged furtive glances and livened up, feeling tension that was joyful not because one of them had been beaten but because they could finally take off the mask of decorum for a short while and admit that marriage was not such a pleasant thing. Yes, those confessions always ended the same way: the oldest of them would philosophically note that it was a woman's lot, and all men had been like that from time immemorial. The women would go silent and then, five minutes later, again wear the masks of decent, happy wives.

There was one incident that struck me more than the rest, though. This was the story of my father's friend's second wife. Since my mother was forbidden to socialize with anyone outside the house, essentially all her friends were the wives of my father's friends. And one of his friends was a bigamist. When I was little I didn't think about what that meant; I was just surprised that he always arrived with two women. The picture became clearer over time, as if I'd finally put on glasses with the right corrective lenses. My father's friend didn't love his second wife and had married her under parental duress: his parents didn't approve of the Russian woman he had chosen for himself and thought that only a young woman from their native land was capable of becoming a worthy wife. I saw how difficult things were for her: she didn't know Russian at all and her puffy eyes were often red from tears during visits, but she always smiled. When his daughter, who was my friend, turned seven, he brought the whole family to Azerbaijan. We got together every year when we visited Baku. They lived outside the city in a huge two-story house, where his first wife lived on the first floor and the second wife lived on the second floor. During one of our trips, we went to visit the second wife after learning she had attempted suicide. When the men were out on the balcony and all the women were in the kitchen, she started talking and spoke for several hours about the seamy side of their marriage, how he beat her, insulted her, refused to be in the same room with her, and called her ugly and fat. I then witnessed a woman violating the well-known fundamental commandment *ev bizim sirr bizim*, Azerbaijani for "our house, our secret." After she stopped speaking, everyone sat, crushed by the pain she had lived with all those years. Nobody dared speak, but what could you say, anyway? Mama just quietly stroked her back, as people stroke children and pets. There was a message beyond love in that gesture: I know what you're talking about.

I've never been able to keep quiet, so when my sister and I got older, I threw myself into protecting my mother and told my father everything she couldn't say. My father didn't answer; he just firmly clenched his teeth in rage and his eyes conveyed only one thought: he knew someone like me would cause problems. He didn't say anything when he found out about my diagnosis. I don't think he understood what was happening until the door of the neurological surgery department slammed behind his back. What was most difficult for him to grasp wasn't the thought of my sickly body, but the very fact that I was now unlikely to become a bride and unlikely to fulfill my parents' wishes. Who needed damaged goods?

When the panic attacks and the first manifestations of my illness began, Bibi attempted to do something about it by bringing me to the mosque. We rode a long time along the shoreline and finally saw the long fingers of minarets. Inside, in a crowded little room, there sat an imam with large, meek eyes that seemed bottomless, gleaming like red lights on the roofs of tall buildings. I held out a few manats for him and he asked who we were praying for; I said my own name. Then we went into a distant, low-ceilinged room where women crowded at the doors, telling one another about their misfortunes, the things that brought them there, their sick daughters and sons, and their problems with sleep and the heart. When the door finally opened, I saw a women wearing a black headscarf and holding a white-hot poker in her hands. The women ahead of me didn't seem to be here for the first time. They calmly lay down on the bright-red rug that decorated the empty space and then periodically lifted the hems of their dresses and tops, closing their eyes as the attendant lowered the tip of the scorching poker and touched it to their ankles, first the left, then the right; their bellies, first on the left, then the right; and finally their necks. When my turn came, I lay down and closed my eyes because I didn't want to see the scorching metal graze my skin, but I was surprised to feel no pain at all. After the ritual, the woman in the black headscarf led me out of the mosque, brought me to the edge of a precipice, and told me to turn so my back was toward the precipice. Hands then smashed two green glass water bottles against each other and I heard someone reciting suras from the Koran. Tiny shards scattered, leaving the sound of destruction while I felt my legs shake and hands on my back. The vibrations subsided when I opened my eyes: deceptive stillness had returned to the air. The woman wearing the black headscarf assured Bibi and me that my body was now healthy because they'd banished the fear inhabiting it by smashing it like those bottles.

The woman in the black headscarf had lied: the illness didn't go anywhere, it methodically took away everything that had ever belonged to me, and several years later, left me a legacy of pain. If something hurt, I didn't tell my parents: this was my pain, my narrative, which I didn't want to share with anyone. To a large extent it's thanks to the illness that they stopped asking when I was finally going to get married, though they still blushed when others asked questions. My body wasn't free of pain, but it had freed me from fulfilling my duty. At some point, even my mute back stopped keeping quiet and shouted to me about our family history, turning it into crumpled papyrus. My muscles cramped so much it was as if someone was wringing out laundry: first the trapezius muscles, later the rhomboid major and rhomboid minor muscles, and then the muscle that went up to my shoulder blade. That pain was incomparable. Maybe it was the pain of all the women in my family: my father's paternal grandmother, whose husband thrashed her out of jealousy; my paternal grandmother, whose husband thrashed her out of jealousy; my mother, whose husband thrashed her out of jealousy. How much pain was hidden in the bruises underneath their scarves? Sometimes the pain wouldn't let me stand up, so I'd lie in bed, entreating some unknown force to stop it.

The muscles in my body were distorted because they didn't work properly: my torso listed to the right like a bent tree, my right arm dangled like a dead wire, and I had trouble breathing. That improved after the operation, but the pain didn't go away completely, returning periodically to remind me who actually controls this body.

IX

LEGS

I RARELY SAW MY MOTHER'S LEGS because they were usually hidden securely beneath fabric, under long skirts and dresses, since legs were not to be displayed, something I'd known since I was a schoolgirl. Length was the main criterion when choosing a dress or skirt, and whenever we bought new clothes, they had to be shown to my father for approval. The older I got, the wider the chasm grew between me and my Russian classmates: I dreamily contemplated their short shorts, miniskirts, and minidresses, knowing I couldn't wear that sort of clothing. Even now, as an adult, I feel uncomfortable if the hem of a skirt, pair of shorts, or dress is above the knee.

The legs of the women around me were not intended for display because they needed to be reliably hidden from strangers' eyes and move slowly around the home, which meant I never saw them running or swimming. My cousins who lived at the seashore never swam. None of them ever swam, even on the hottest days, when they silently sat at the water's edge in long skirts or summer trousers. My sister and I, who grew up far from the sea, rushed to take off our T-shirts and skirts, and immediately dashed into the water, diving in headfirst, cheerfully splashing, enjoying the cool water and bright patches of sunlight as our cousins silently observed from the shore.

Since there were rules to follow, choosing a swimsuit always took several hours. The bottom needed to cover the entire bikini area and hips, so my mother frequently chose shorts rather than the typical panty-like swimsuit bottoms. Décolletage was strictly forbidden: the swimsuit should be a one-piece with a neckline all the way to the throat, and it should cover the chest and back. Bikinis weren't even contemplated and Mama strove to walk past them as quickly as possible, hurrying my sister and me along. However, we still managed to touch the mysterious little bra-like tops and bottoms of various shapes and colors, sewn from polyester and Lycra.

At the beach, we encountered women in glamorous bikinis, which were exciting objects of envy for us. The hot sand didn't burn those women's feet as they walked calmly along, proudly looking at those around them, certain of their own beauty. I was glad for the existence of women like that—proud, beautiful, and not shy about their bodies—while also realizing that the body is similar to sand: pliant muscles quickly lose their form, too, affirming the value of savoring one's youth. Of course, my women relatives disagreed with me and I could hear dissatisfied sounds as the syllables of the word *tərbiyəsiz*, "uncouth" or "ill-bred," rolled out. I initially attempted to argue with them, sincerely wondering why they found female bodies in bikinis so outrageous. Could a swimsuit really make a woman depraved or unworthy of respect? But I soon let that thought go because I realized that disaffected whispering was a mode of communication for them, a permissible means of solidarity. By condemning the bodies of strangers, they consoled their own bodies, which were eternally and prudishly closed off and hidden by fabric. It was difficult for them to admit that they also couldn't singlehandedly retain control over their own bodies, just as they couldn't stop existing as the objects of social pressure, others' desires, and male power. Yes, of course there were among them women who voluntarily cloaked their bodies, adhering to their own convictions and religion. But most of them looked ruefully at beautiful bikinis and shimmering dresses that they couldn't wear because they now belonged to men whose will was equal to Allah's. On the other hand, I thought, who said that a body in a swimsuit isn't the equal of a body in a long dress? At what point did people decide that an exposed female body is sexier and more interesting than a covered body? Was my body in a long skirt really not as beautiful as my classmates' bodies in short skirts? I had more and more questions as I got older, but I couldn't ask my mother or my aunt since we never talked about the body. The very topic was considered shameful, as if we had no bodies at all, remembering them only when some part wasn't functioning as it should.

I thought my body was abnormal until I went to a public swimming pool. I was shocked at the number of partially exposed women's bodies around me because I had never seen so many scantily clad women in one place. It was a genuine revelation and relief to realize how varied and imperfect bodies are. Not one body that I saw at the pool resembled those I'd seen in magazines or on the screen. The bodies at the pool were alive and pulsing—full-figured and thin, young and old—and they were all interesting, just like books. No two wrinkles or creases were the same; breasts, as they should, sagged slightly, and legs were strewn with Martian craters of cellulite. But the important thing was that nobody paid attention to my bare body; nobody was interested in my big hips, the ugly mole on my left breast, my rounded belly, or my bruises and scars: my body was an ordinary woman's body, susceptible to age and biological processes. Seeing the bodies of others means seeing one's own as it actually is: unadorned and lacking additional meanings. Serene female bodies at the pool—white, porcelain, almost transparent skin with a sprinkling of reddish moles; firm and slightly yellowish skin with drops of water; dark skin resembling kraft paper—all told stories about what it means for women's bodies to change, gain weight, and become covered with spots, scratches, and scars. Their bodies' statements were equivalent. There was no comparing them and they didn't look like the bodies at beaches. They were distinguished by serenity because at the pool you needn't worry that your body would be judged or assessed, and nobody was interested in a new swimsuit or a flat stomach since this was a place where the body didn't need to appear to be anything more than it was. Just like in hospital wards, where bodies are simply bodies, a form of existence and empathy, a conversation without a conversation.

Since my father didn't like us to bare our bodies in public, we swam in the sea for no more than an hour. He herded us back into the car as soon as everyone had taken a dip and eaten the routine number of watermelon slices. When we got home, we quickly washed off the sea salt, changed into summer dresses, and went out on the veranda, where Bibi, my father's second sister, was already setting the table. While the men sat around the table and finished their evening cigarettes, we helped arrange dishes of *üç bacı*,[18] moistened dry white lavash with water so it would soften, and cut fresh tomatoes and cucumbers into big pieces.

All the women in my family knew the rule—don't bare your legs—and never violated it, so even the clothes we wore at home had to cover the legs as well as the breasts. Mama joked that this was the best way to hide cellulite. Once when we were getting ready for a wedding, I learned by accident that there can be cellulite on a woman's legs. Mama was standing in her underwear and choosing what to wear. I had my first close look at her legs and saw they were covered in strange dents that looked like the trail of a fallen comet. I remember feeling scared: Was it normal that her legs were changing? Would my legs be like that, too?

---

18 "Three sisters" (Azerbaijani). This traditional Azerbaijani dish consists of peppers, tomatoes, and eggplants stuffed with meat and herbs.

My body, which had once been firmly attached to my mother's by an umbilical cord, was covered in its own dents. Immediately after surgery, my body became more and more like my mother's, as if deferring death had allowed it to finally recall its own ancestry. I gained fifteen kilograms in just a year as my body became large, unwieldy, and unattractive; old jeans and pretty dresses no longer fit. I searched a long time for the size I needed, crying in the dressing room if I realized that yet another pair of trousers wouldn't slide over my enlarged hips. I inherited them from my mother. They were broad and bulky, resembling two stones, making it difficult for me to find trousers since they were either too small at the top or baggy down below. I mourned the ease with which I used to buy things without a second thought. My body was getting larger and heavier, though, gravitating toward the ground as if it knew that was where it would eventually end up.

Dystonia first destroyed my right foot. Walking became more difficult with every passing day: each step brought pain, the foot didn't position itself properly, and spasms always made it clench and turn inward like an embryo. The doctors shrugged their shoulders, prescribed orthopedic inserts, and recommended massage, but time went on and the foot still ached in pain. Then my whole right leg stopped responding: it constantly crumpled from endless cramps, and I felt my muscles arbitrarily contracting and pulsing. My right leg stiffened, hardened, and lost the ability to bend, as if it were filled with cement. I got a cane when walking became difficult.

My first cane was utterly ordinary, a folding stick from the pharmacy that a friend brought me. It was easier to walk with the cane because I could lean on it without being afraid I'd fall, but my mother's eyes filled with tears whenever she saw it. She begged me not to take the cane with me because she didn't want anyone to see me with it. My parents tried to hide my illness, perhaps in the hope that it would disappear. Or maybe they hadn't lost hope that their elder daughter would marry after all. Healthy young women were taken more readily as wives, so I wasn't to display my unhealthy body. Speaking of my illness meant cutting off the future they wished for me, cutting myself off from a world of other women within the diaspora and the culture, and becoming akin to a disgraceful, amputated limb.

The second cane was almost a luxury item. It was bewitching, with a long handle carved out of beech from the Caucasus. It was black, with tongues of flame, though it was also very awkward. For one thing, the handle was higher than my waist, which impeded my walking, and, second, it didn't fold and was very heavy. But I liked that cane, mostly because it served as a reminder of a past love, a reminder that any stranger is a potential lover. My mother didn't care for that cane either; she insisted I not use any cane. I thought that neither she nor my father fully realized the seriousness of my illness, that they barely believed it existed, that it seemed temporary to them, like a cold or insomnia. They also didn't understand something I'd grasped immediately: their healthy little girl was gone, never to return.

Every second of every minute of every day I could feel the illness destroying my former body. When I woke up, I'd sense yet another twisted muscle, contractions pressing my chest cavity, my arms tangling like seaweed, and my right leg becoming shorter than the left because of spasms and muscle atrophy. Worst of all were the moments of dystonic attack, also known as dystonic storms. That English-language term is very apt since the speed with which you lose control truly does resemble a storm or hurricane. All the muscles start clenching as if there'd been a signal from a conductor's invisible baton: one wave of the baton and your mouth stretches downward or to the right like melting ice cream; a second wave and your head tilts downward and freezes as if someone won't stop pulling your hair; and with the baton's third wave your hands are clenched like a crowned eagle's talons clutching captured prey. To an observer, this scene recalls an exorcism. Maybe the possessed were actually dystonic, and their unnaturally bent backs were the result of extensive cramping. Of course, we'll never find out. In the neurological departments that I visited periodically, the hallways were always lined with metal handrails to help patients get around without falling. My legs could barely move, as if they were enshrouded in a numbing sleep and had turned to stone. My right foot dragged along the floor, making a sound that distantly resembled the rustling of autumn leaves. Nobody in the neurological department cared about the beauty of legs since they were focused on how legs bent at the knees, the workings of the hip's quadricep muscle and the shin's triceps surae muscles, how muscles reacted to touch and accomplished their primary purpose, and if the body moved with the requisite diligence and responsiveness.

Because of the illness and my foot's failure to position itself properly, I couldn't wear heels, which I'd never particularly liked. But I began dreaming of them just as I lost the opportunity to wear them without a thought. I looked in fascination at dressy footwear in shoe stores, gazed enviously at women who strode with confidence, and joyfully listened to the characteristic clack of heels inside buildings. I decided that after the operation I had to buy myself some red high-heeled shoes that clacked when I walked.

My feet were wound in elastic bandages after the operation. They lay calmly on the hospital bed, waiting for when they'd again need to stand and walk. The bandages swaddled them like a blanket embraces a newborn. When I was allowed to stand, I immediately felt the lack of pain and knew that my muscles were simply doing their work, as if they had finally been freed. It turned out that the mere ability to walk was more interesting than heels, so I bought myself some sneakers instead.

X
THROAT

DURING WEDDINGS, women's long, beautiful necks displayed jewelry for all to see: collar-length, matinee-length, opera-length, and other chains that absolutely needed to be gold strewn with precious stones. Those pieces of jewelry bore messages from one woman to another, telling of a husband's love, of an engagement, of an argument, or of redemption after guilt. Nobody shared the history of their jewelry, but observers usually figured it out as if it were part of a cryptic scene in an art house movie. Mama didn't like beads and necklaces, but she set aside money from her salary to buy herself beautiful silver rings. She gave one to me: silver with white and pink cubic zirconia in a size that fit only my ring finger. It doesn't suit me at all, but I always take it with me and sometimes put it on so I can feel the connection between us. Mama has never worn the pearl necklace she inherited from her mother, my grandmother; it lay in a brown box that she brought from Georgia.

My maternal grandmother never took off the fragile necklace made of wild pearls that lay on her dark skin right up until the moment the neighbor women washed her tired body and wrapped it in a dense white shroud. They gave the pearl necklace to her daughter as an eternal reminder that jewelry tells its own stories after its owner's death. My grandmother was often feverish from cancer and her throat constricted in attacks of shortness of breath; she would open all the windows in her little bedroom and lie on the floor below them. When she periodically struggled from pain at night, she went out on the balcony and admired Georgia's night sky. The Georgian sky was more beautiful than anything I'd ever seen: the full moon hung low over the Earth, like the pupil of an eye you could easily touch with your finger if you jumped. Night covered the small Georgian village in dense darkness, as if someone had gently pressed a heavenly light switch. Stars winked at one another, conveying entire poems in Morse code to local residents but remaining undeciphered. My grandmother wordlessly observed the celestial bodies from her heavenly coffin, watching as their glistening white shrouds stopped radiating light when they began merging with the darkness. She knew this fate awaited everyone on Earth but felt sorry she wouldn't be able to sew clothes, tapping away at the pedal of her sewing machine. There were no sounds in her coffin—it was a place where speech had returned to the Creator.

My paternal grandmother didn't wear jewelry. She usually draped a kerchief around her neck when she went to pick basil and other herbs. Under the Azerbaijani sun, little droplets of sweat quickly coated her neck. In the evenings, they gave way to scattered weariness and regrets since at the end of each workday she thought she could have done more. And she would fall asleep, sighing lightly in disappointment. Night quickly covered the slopes of the Zangilan Mountains, eroding their peaks and shading the contours of the trees as the world blurred like a shoreline after a tsunami. When she was sure there were no witnesses, my paternal grandmother would whisper a nocturnal prayer: the words bumped into one another as if they were clumped prayer beads that then skittered down through her voice box. Only once did she miss the prayer. When she opened her mouth to begin speaking on the night of her death, she realized that her words had listlessly draped over her vocal chords and returned to the Creator.

Women preferred not to speak out loud: all their complaints, curses at men, and regrets about lives that had passed too quickly without being adequately understood were packed into prayers that they sent in whispers to an unknown addressee. They felt better in the morning after the prayer because it seemed as if the words that had been released into the world took that burden with them. I often heard my mother pray at night.

My mother and I had to sleep in the same bed after my operation. When my mother thought I was sleeping at night, she would begin to pray, telling Allah about all her suffering and fears, and requesting his protection. It felt strange to be an adult sleeping in the same bed as a parent. Bodies deprived of their previous lightness and connection tossed and turned ponderously, trying to avoid chance contact. We thought about different things after turning away from each other. I could barely sleep. I wasn't supposed to lie on my stomach because of the stimulator that had been implanted in me, but I couldn't sleep on my back. The stitches itched and I had trouble turning my neck as it attempted to come to terms with the alien presence of the wire. Every cell of my skin sensed the stimulator: I felt its bulging metal edges and its heaviness; I could also sense my body failing to accept it and I felt pain in my skull from the metal staples. My mother was, yet again, mentally reviewing her life, both the past and the possible future, and asking herself the question: Might her life have turned out differently?

Only a month later did my body adjust to the presence of the metal object inside it and stop reacting. Once I'd healed, I barely knew the stimulator was there, and it needed only weekly charging and two tune-ups a year. When I was allowed to walk after the operation, the neurosurgeon led me to a small white room filled with small white coffin-like boxes on floor-to-ceiling shelves. He took down a box at random and held it out to me. I remember the trepidation I felt when I carried it into the ward like a New Year's gift; I didn't know then that the box and I would never be apart for even one day, that I would take it with me on trips and make sure it lay in a clean, dry place. From now on, my capacity to function lay in that little box: a base station for the adaptor, the adaptor itself, a cord, a few types of plugs, two collars for cordless charging, instructions in several languages, and a remote control. The box was completely white, and the inscription Model DB-6412-EU-C Vercise Charging System flaunted itself almost cheerfully. The neurologist went through a brief instructional session, showing what the buttons on the remote did: red was on/off for the system, P was on/off for the remote, the button with a silhouette of a person selected the proper program, and the up and down arrows adjusted the level of current. I thought about how funny it was that I now had a remote control for myself, though it was even funnier that I'd become dependent on electricity, meaning that my plan to buy a little house in the middle of nowhere would remain unfulfilled.

When I went for a tune-up a month after the operation, the hallway was unusually lively, and the comfortable black couch next to the nurse's station was full of patients. Each patient held a remote control that looked like mine. When the neurologist came into the hallway, she pushed up her glasses and sternly ordered that nobody switch on their remotes. It turned out that they were all manufactured by Boston Scientific Corporation and could control any stimulator within range, so it was theoretically possible to mistakenly adjust a neighbor's stimulator rather than one's own. After a short wait, I went into the doctor's office. She connected my stimulator to a tablet and warned that she was now going to change my settings. A moment later, my eyes darkened, strange colored blotches appeared, and my right hand cramped and spasmed. The doctor silently looked at me and changed the settings back. Another minute later and the whole right side of my body cramped and I couldn't open my mouth, which was taut as a thread. She looked at me again and readjusted the settings. After a couple more unsuccessful attempts, she finally found a frequency where I maintained my functionality; she then asked me to walk around the department for twenty minutes or so. She had essentially controlled my body, almost as if it were a toy car: the buttons on her tablet determined if I'd be able to speak, move my hands and legs freely, see, and lead a full life. My body had become as functional and controllable as a household appliance, but existential horror had been replaced by endless worries over technological viability. What if the adaptor broke or the remote got wet? Would the stimulator really last for twenty-five years or would it suddenly malfunction prematurely? I was even afraid to bathe the first week, but the neurologist assured me that everything was fine. On airplanes, I take the stimulator's little white box in my carry-on luggage and press it to my chest when there's turbulence; on trains I keep it under my pillow; at home I put it in a chest of drawers after making sure it's completely dry. The little white box and the metal object sewn around my collarbone have practically become family members. I'm always afraid that if there's a fire or the building collapses I won't have time to grab the box and will always remain locked in my own disintegrating body, unable to close my mouth.

After coming home from the neurological center, I wore a hat or scarf, though not because I was embarrassed about my shaved head; I'd almost gotten used to the absence of hair because it made daily life easier. I didn't need to wash my hair, worry about how it looked, comb anything, contrive hairstyles, or buy barrettes and bobby pins. The only downside was that it was very cold, and it seemed as if a lot of warmth escaped through my scalp. I wore headscarves because my mother demanded it; she was afraid that people would see my maimed head, the seven scars smudged with green antiseptic and the metal staples that held together the pieces of my skull. She didn't think the world should know I was sick.

And it's true: the world didn't need to know how my body was falling apart, how it was ceasing to function, how terribly the stitches itched, or how the stitching under my collarbone had covered itself in a white crust while healing. But by negating my body, I was also negating a layer of my historical and cultural inheritance, not accepting my own impermanence, and not admitting the eternal connection of my body with the bodies of other women. I wanted to finally break the vicious circle of retribution and open our shut mouths so I could shout about my own existence and the existences of mothers, grandmothers, sisters, and girlfriends. We'd been clutching each other by the throat, in a death grip of fear, for too long—*but what if someone sees, but what if someone finds out, but what will people say, but what will your relatives think, but what will your father do when he finds out*—and an unbreakable chain of horror had held us by the throat for years, suffocating us, just as dystonia had suffocated me.

Sometimes I think about how symbolic my illness turned out to be: the more muscles my illness occupied, the less freedom I had. In addition to my speech defects, at some point I began having difficulty swallowing and breathing, so little pieces of food went down the wrong pipe whenever I ate. This started happening more and more often, so I started eating less and drinking more because it felt as if my body was refusing food. My body was withering from dystonic attacks, listlessly drifting off to sleep and only capable of swallowing liquids: water, coffee, juice, and soup. During intense attacks, I'd feel my throat shrink when air had trouble forcing its way between muscles seized by spasms, and my mouth would open and attempt to take in as much air as possible, as if I were swimming with my head down and had suddenly realized there was nothing left to breathe.

Those regular attacks left my body as relaxed as a deflated air mattress; I even lacked the strength to turn from one side to the other, so I just lay on my back like a drowning victim who'd been pulled from the water and was glad to be able to breathe. Air calmly slid down my throat and dispersed throughout my lungs. I thought about how nice it was to have a throat, larynx, and vocal cords that could freely and easily pronounce words. Words changed places, attracting and repelling one another; they not only proclaimed the fact of my existence, but were also a reservoir of tenderness, grief, and joy, conveying secret knowledge through my mother's prayers, fairy tales, warnings, recipes, confessions, and even curses.

XI

BELLY

I DON'T REMEMBER WHEN MY FLAT, child's belly changed forever and became huge and jelly-like, like my mother's. I knew that the belly was the most important part of a woman's body because that's where babies placidly lie, head down, like holiday decorations. When Mama was pregnant with a son, everyone around her worried about her belly, stroked it, looked at it, touched it—everyone knew what was behind the wall of her belly, in her uterus, and that she was carrying the most valuable thing a woman can carry. Her belly grew larger each day, rounding like a snail's shell so even an old appendicitis scar looked festive on her taut skin.

After my mother's pregnant belly came the pregnant bellies of two cousins who rapidly married, one right after the other. Pregnant bellies replaced wedding dresses with such speed that I didn't even have a chance to congratulate them about their weddings before babies' due dates started approaching. My mother's face grew gloomy whenever she found out about her nieces' pregnancies. Of course she was happy for them, but she was also upset that I wasn't planning to marry or have children, and it pained her that all the preparations for the niece brides and even the ritual of bringing these brides out of their father's house took place in our apartment. My mother's sister had divorced her husband—she was the only woman I knew who had enough courage to leave a husband who beat her, taking four children with her—and I respected her for that. Someone thus had to substitute for the father figure and since their apartment was smaller, they decided the girls would leave our house to marry. That made my mother and father all the more distressed since they'd been waiting for the moment when I'd step out our doorway wearing a frilly dress with a red ribbon at the waist, to the sounds of "Vagzaly."

The topics at women's gatherings in the kitchen changed as we grew up. They were initially conversations about schools and universities, but they quickly transformed into discussion of more urgent matters: weddings and children. When aunts, relatives, and my mother's girlfriends met, it was obvious from their greetings that the tone had changed because they noted that I'd grown up and become beautiful. They then coyly tossed in phrases like "such a bride already," or "soon it will be time for you to marry." When guests came, my mother monitored what I wore, how I behaved, and how I spoke (including how loudly), and she corrected my behavior much more strictly than before. I'd already reached marriageable age after all, meaning that anyone who came to our house could see me as a potential bride.

All the unmarried women at weddings wished they could find that happiness, too, and candies were placed in their hands: that candy absolutely had to be eaten unless they wanted to deprive themselves of the joy of becoming a bride. A wedding, after all, was the culmination of becoming a woman. The subject changed as soon as the festive occasion was over: When would the children start coming, why weren't there children, and who exactly was unfit, the husband or the wife? If a child was born, the women discussed what the baby looked like, how healthy they were, and when the newlyweds would plan to have a second. There was never a shortage of topics.

Over the course of several years, all my female cousins ended up married with children, and they were proud and almost defiant when they came to gatherings: they'd managed to fulfill their primary daughterly mission. They tossed haughty, pitying glances my way because, in their opinion, I wasn't a full-fledged woman at all since I'd decided not to marry and not to have children, despite being nearly thirty, which was my last chance by diaspora standards. We'd fallen out of touch over the years and they saw no need to converse with a woman who hadn't managed to punctually marry and have children, and I saw that they regarded me as a blot on our family or a mishap in a community for which discussing an errant life was considered more enjoyable than admitting a repulsive truth.

Sadly, we were never particularly close except when we were very little, before we'd been burdened by the weight of responsibility and social stereotypes; in years gone by, we tightly embraced each other in family photographs. I periodically see pretty pictures on Instagram with dogs, children, and husbands, where there's no sign of family quarrels or slaps, no disclosures of unfaithfulness, and no whiff of hostility—all that is securely hidden from outsiders' eyes. If something happens—a husband's infidelity or violence—it's quickly crumpled up and tossed into the dirty laundry. And then washed, ironed, and worn again, looking its very best. The house seethes with discussion for a couple of days, but things always end the same way: divorce is impossible and it's natural for men to err. The older women affirm that's how things have always been; you can't change a man's nature and there's no use becoming a divorcée unless the situation is extreme.

My cousins snoop on my sinful life through the social media peephole, too, judging my decisions and gossiping. The longer I stay an unmarried, childless woman, the surer I am that I'll never stop being the focus of widespread discussion and disapproval. It's as if syllables from the roomy words *ka-dın, qa-dın, zhen-shchin-a*[19] will be dropped if no wedding ring appears on a woman's finger and her womb never carries a child. I know that I'm no longer a true woman to them and they all slyly look away, ironically asking during family dinners about work, as if I'd written the wrong answer on the blackboard or hadn't learned the most important lesson at school.

What does it mean to be a woman in our family? Do I stop being a woman if I decline the role of mother and wife, and

---

19 "Woman" in Turkish, Azeri, and Russian, respectively.

will I stop being part of the culture, the history, and the diaspora if parts of my body remember their origins? And is it really necessary to reproduce and continue the family line in order to have a heritage?

The bellies of the women I knew both united and separated them. The first unifying event was, of course, menstruation. That topic, though, was considered taboo, meaning nobody ever talked about it at home. And so, when I was twelve years old, I discovered a strange dark-brown liquid with a tinge of maroon on my panties and decided I was dying. I put in some toilet paper and walked around for half an hour, hoping it would stop. But nothing went away. I then decided it was cancer, since that, after all, was the only illness I knew of. I went to my mother and announced, through trembling lips, that I was dying. When she realized what had happened, my mother held out a sanitary napkin and left the room. The only thing she told me on the subject was that under no circumstances should I use tampons because only married women used them. At some point, I found out that all the women around me menstruated—my cousins, aunts, other relatives, and girlfriends—but nobody talked about it. It was as if this was our shared crime, and confessing to it would certainly bring punishment and judgment. Women gave advice from time to time on medications or which pads to use so as not to ruin the mattress. But I learned the most from *Everything for Girls*, a big pink encyclopedia that contained an entire chapter dedicated to a girl's maturation. Yes, its language was florid and not always straightforward, but one thing was clear: menstruation made motherhood possible.

It was very painful whenever it came: my lower abdomen cramped, bright-red blood didn't seem to stop flowing for a second, and each month, along with the blood, my body bid farewell to a lost child as well as to my formerly carefree, unburdened body that didn't need to reproduce in order to avoid death. My mother sternly monitored our home to ensure there was nothing in sight that would indicate the critical days, so as to prevent my father from accidentally seeing pads or other attributes of his daughters' maturing bodies in the bathroom.

I was relieved when I found out that my classmates had periods, too. We helped each other out in the girl's locker rooms and bathrooms by keeping an eye on our friends' trousers and skirts and pointing out if a bright-red spot appeared on the fabric. We were accomplices. We thought up secret names for what was happening to us because it couldn't be spoken of out loud: *red days on the calendar, those days, guests, code red, it started*, and *they started*, and we whispered about it to each other as if we were taking turns burying a corpse in the forest. Why weren't we allowed to say this out loud? Maybe because that made us vulnerable around men who now knew we could be mothers? Or maybe saying the word *menstruation* aloud shattered the crystal pedestals of the past on which there stood fragile female bodies of white porcelain, captivating with their beauty or gently holding a bundle with a newborn baby that appeared who-knew-how from who-knew-where? Whatever the case, there was to be no talk about one's own body, about what was happening to it, if it was ill or healthy, gaining or losing weight—the body had to be invisible and nothing drew more attention than a crimson bloodstain.

In the world where I grew up, men were only glad to see a woman's blood on their wedding night. They longed not only to see proof of a woman's virginity but also to possess the bloodstained evidence that she had been irrevocably given to them. Though many refused the tradition of hanging out a white sheet with a spot for all to see, everyone knew that was an obligatory part of the ritual: the groom could return his bride at any moment if she didn't meet his expectations. It was as if the virginal hymen were a sheep that had to be sacrificed in order to prove one's love.

Once my parents came to visit me in the hospital, at the very beginning of my treatment. I went out to the hallway to see them while wearing leggings and a white sweater, the most comfortable and typical hospital clothing. We talked for fifteen or twenty minutes and as they were leaving, my mother said I should put on trousers because my father was angry. My body angered him and my legs in tight-fitting fabric interested him more than his own drunkenness, more than the illness that had ruined my health, and more than my mother's misfortune; they angered him because they were visible. Visibility for a woman was only tolerated during

MY DREADFUL BODY

pregnancy, and even then, her round belly evidenced not only impending motherhood but also belonging to a man, an eternal bond with the one who chose her to be his wife. I had again violated the rules.

When the spasms in my belly first began, I didn't initially know what they were, thinking they were just menstruation. But they didn't go away and only worsened, so I called for an ambulance, thinking I had appendicitis. A neurologist finally told me it was most likely muscle spasms in my belly. I was used to pain, but whenever new pain arrived, I needed time to get used to it, to learn how to recognize it and coexist with it. It was as if I opened my eyes every morning to find that adopted children had shown up in the house. That meant another room would now be occupied. But words and pain took up the space instead of children. And they were all that fully belonged to me, since words and pain were as impossible to take or give away as the rocks of Gobustan.[20]

When my mother's labor contractions started, she didn't initially know what they were because the date was too early. I was supposed to be born on December 25, but I was born on October 27, the first day of her maternity leave. It wasn't my mother's hands that greeted me into this world but cold metal forceps that indifferently grasped my newborn head. Since I was kept in a neonatal incubator for several days, my

---

[20] Gobustan is an archaeological reserve in Azerbaijan, south of Baku, where there are petroglyphs dating from the early Paleolithic era until the Middle Ages on a rocky plateau between the southeastern slope of the Greater Caucasus and the Caspian Sea.

mother didn't pick me up until a few days later, meaning that the very first hands present in my life were my father's. The doctors advised my parents not to give their child—who was too small and might not survive—a name, but they (more specifically, my father) named me. They decided that if they were to choose an Azerbaijani word—*yeganə*, meaning "the only one"—they could outsmart the world, which would yield to the magic of words and spare my life. That small, already named body learned to breathe and gained weight without suspecting that its early arrival was no accident. I was not a first child; I was their second, but the first had not survived. The first, the non-survivor, had not even had a chance to form before leaving my mother's body after my father's kick. Not even pregnancy tamed my father's jealousy: rage overcame him the way a caring mother covers her child from head to toe with a blanket. Continually convinced of her unfaithfulness, my father had kicked my mother in the belly, unaware that his rage had already cost another's life. He repented after each outburst of rage: he was ashamed and wanted to make amends for the guilt, so he would become more attentive and considerate, bringing home stray cats and dogs in his winter jacket. It was as if saving homeless animals might rehabilitate him.

The doctors gathered before my operation to attempt to figure out when the dystonia first appeared, what could have provoked it, and what type it was—they wanted to try to unravel the tangle of medical screenings done over the last three years. We first ruled out dopamine-responsive dystonia after they gave me a small dose of levodopa and sent me into a narrow white hallway of the regional hospital; the neurologist told me three times not to go anywhere. I had never felt the way I did then. Though I could stand, my eyes seemed to be stuck together and my whole body was becoming simultaneously soft and hard, like a stone sinking in water. They then sent me to Moscow, to the only laboratory where it was possible to do an analysis for mutations in the DYT1, DYT6, DYT5, and DYT12 genes, to rule out an inherited type of dystonia. Once they'd ruled that out, too, the doctors presumed that the dystonia had developed due to hypoxia in the brain at birth. My father's rage had yet again flowed over my mother's body like lava, provoking the birth of a child incapable of breathing independently while damaging her brain and mutilating her body forever. True, nobody knew about that at the time, as my mother placidly rocked the baby and quietly sang a traditional Azeri lullaby:

Laylay, balam, yatasan,
Sleep, child, do sleep,

> In a world
> Where only dreams belong to you

Qızılgülə batasan.
May you drown in roses.

> Save them for the long winter

Gül yastığın içində
Şirin yuxu tapasan.
May you find sweet dreams
On a pillow of flowers.

> Your body is not yours at all
> It is the body of mothers and fathers

Laylay, laylay, a laylay,
Körpə balam, a laylay.
Sleep, my little one, bayu-by.

> Sleep is the road to paradise
> There, nothing at all will hurt
> There your mother will never shout

Laylay, beşiyim, laylay
Evim-eşiyim, laylay.
Sən get şirin yuxuya,
Çəkim keşiyin, laylay.
Sleep, my baby in your cradle, bayu-by,
You are all that I have:
My home, my hearth, do sleep.
Go have sweet dreams,
And I'll protect your sleep 'til dawn.

> You are my home but I can ruin it
> Because I'm the one who birthed you

MY DREADFUL BODY

Laylay, laylay, a laylay,
Körpə balam, a laylay.
Sleep, my little one, bayu-by.

    I will love you as long
    As your body stays small and your soul is still strong
    But when your body exceeds the size of your soul
    Well, that's when disaster's foretold

    As they fly over Guba,[21] the birds
    See your father
    As he drives to his parents to visit
    He's wound words 'round his fist

    From all the women in their line:
    Mother, wife, daughters, the elder, the younger,
    And amidst them,
    There calmly runs a mountain stream

    That is where all our bodies lie.

---

21 Guba is a city in northern Azerbaijan.

TRANSLATOR'S NOTE

READING AND TRANSLATING Egana Djabbarova's *My Dreadful Body* has been one of my most affecting and interesting Russophone reading experiences in recent years. Translating the book has been an intricate task but I'm a translator who yearns for "intricate." In this slender but powerful work, Djabbarova shifts and shuffles languages, themes, and literary devices so deftly that the text coalesces into an almost encyclopedic guide to the narrator's life.

I tend to be a "love at first sight" reader and the opening pages of *My Dreadful Body* drew me right in. The narrator, Egana, describes cousins—all girls and women—sitting together in Azerbaijan as the "grown women" of the group pluck one another's eyebrows. Sisterhood is literal here since Russian cousins are essentially sisters or brothers once removed. Djabbarova skillfully threads the cousins' fraught relationships through eleven chapters, each of which is named for a body part.

The word *fraught* describes Egana's relationships with everything from expectations for female hair and clothing styles to marriage and social graces. Given the fraught nature of all these matters, Egana's frank discussion of her immediate family, the Azerbaijani diaspora community in Russia, patriarchal demands, and serious health issues are hardly welcome. In describing Egana's life and her difficulties negotiating and often rejecting the strictures placed upon her by cultural and religious norms, Djabbarova's writing has an almost schematic—but not at all simplistic—quality, as Egana tells personal stories about her life and family. Her chapters tell of the aforementioned eyebrows (to pluck or not to pluck?) and hair (to cut or not to cut?) and legs (how to cover them?), letting us know how little say she has over her own grooming and choice of clothes. Perhaps the most glorious aspect of Djabbarova's achievement in *My Dreadful Body* is that her intricate weaving of all the novella's elements feels so effortless. Set in Russia, Azerbaijan, and Georgia, her stories flow and flow.

Most of the rules, preferences, and forms of alienation that Egana describes weren't new to me, but as I read and worked, I kept thinking about the concentric circles those elements were forming, starting with the most hidden body parts and thoughts, then continuing on to family matters and the diaspora community's habits of stating opinions and upholding social norms. Meanwhile, Egana yearns for freedom to make her own decisions and speak her mind. Despite large differences in our backgrounds, many readers, like me, will recognize some of their own frustrations and qualities in Egana's: feminism, a propensity for forming and voicing opinions, wishes for a different eye color or hairstyle, family strife, and the trauma of bullying among them.

The motifs and literary devices in *My Dreadful Body* fit together beautifully thanks to Djabbarova's language. As her translator, I am most fascinated by what might seem mundane: the way she combines and arranges her words, particularly since she makes language and form fit so closely with all the topics I've mentioned above. Her writing both creates a certain sense of distance from her narrator, Egana—who remains unnamed until the very end of the book—and makes intimate connections to traumatic incidents. The mastery of Djabbarova's blend of tones, moods, literary devices, and languages felt especially apparent because *My Dreadful Body* is a book that reads easily for me—everything made sense and was clear from the start—but required tremendous patience to translate. I found myself focusing particularly carefully on the sounds of words and the rhythms of sentences—for me, the most intuitive part of translation. I fussed more than usual when choosing words, hoping to coax metaphors to retain their beauty, keep cultural nuances accessible, and allow the cadences of the text to add to the novel's atmosphere. *My Dreadful Body* is short, yes, but I stared out the window a lot—that's a crucial part of translation for me—trying to find the proper words and phrases for delicate imagery and private thoughts. It is a beautiful composition, filled with visceral pain and ugly truths. Having read the book at least ten times between the English and Russian texts, I can say that rich rewards await those who will reread it and discover more and more complexities and connections in Djabbarova's writing.

Perhaps the biggest translation challenges were tied to Djabbarova's propensity for folding non-Russian words into her Russian. In an online presentation about her writing, hosted by Amherst College on May 2, 2025, Djabbarova said, "I never exist in one language." She also dreams in multiple languages. The fact that I also do both of those things—they're part of my identity, too—and tend to think of certain concepts in only one language, made me all the more determined to signal to the reader when the Russian text of *My Dreadful Body* includes non-Russian words. I've strived to at least try to approximate for Anglophone readers the effect the book has on Russophone readers.

Perhaps my favorite non-Russian word in the book is *uzerlik*, a word that's written *üzərlik* in Azeri and appears in Russian as *узерлик*; both words result in the transliteration *uzerlik*. The Russian *uzerlik* seems to exist almost exclusively in conjunction with Azerbaijan, and generated under three thousand hits on Google; Russian has other words for this plant, which is known to English speakers as "wild rue." One of those Russian names for the plant happens to be могильник (pronounced *mogil'nik*), a word that's translated in Oxford's Russian dictionary as "burial ground." Although the footnote for *uzerlik* in the Russian text of *My Dreadful Body* mentions "burial ground," I stuck to the botanical aspect in the English footnote, opting to mention burial grounds here instead. The presence of that meaning is informative in a note for Russophone readers, but it's an interesting bit of trivia that might even be a confusing distraction for an Anglophone reader. *Üzerlik* is also a toponym, for a small town in Türkiye.

The *uzerlik* paragraph in the "Eyes" chapter of *My Dreadful Body* offers other examples of our decision-making for handling Djabbarova's non-Russian words. She invokes wild rue in "Eyes" because Egana's mother burns it as protection against the evil eye. Another form of protection is *göz monjuk*, which is described as "a blue eye with a small black pupil in the middle," often displayed in Azeri homes. That Azeri phrase is described immediately in the text, so there's no need for a footnote. A bit later, however, there's a mention of these eye talismans hanging in stores and studios in "Baku's *İçərişəhər*, the Old City." Though that term was unfamiliar to me—or perhaps simply forgotten since I visited Baku on several trips in the 1990s and wandered the Old City many times—that toponym seems readable enough for Anglophones, thanks to the schwa, so we left it in as is but translated the meaning in the text itself, as a stealth gloss. That felt more fitting and natural for the English translation than recreating the brief footnote in the Russian text. Finally, the same paragraph offers up a rather grisly Azeri phrase—"*Pis gozler partasin pis gozler kor olsun*"—that we handled as the Russian text does. It needed no transliteration for Anglophone readers, but we translated the footnote from the Russian book.

Given that much of *My Dreadful Body* concerns Egana's health, there were numerous medical terms to sort out, too. Although I wasn't familiar with dysarthria or dystonia when I started working on the book, those terms were clear-cut during my first reading since they refer to very specific disorders with names that are nearly identical in Russian and English. Symptoms, though, were often more difficult to describe, given that cramps and spasms are similar yet different, and the boundaries of Russian and English words (which I often picture as Venn diagrams) can have considerable differences and similarities. I also recall from my long-ago experience as a medical interpreter how hard it is to quantify or describe pain in any language. On the technical side, an online manual saved me (I hope!) from errors about the remote control kit that Egana receives for her deep brain stimulator. We did remove many medical footnotes, given that "Parkinson's disease" and "botulinum toxin therapy" are common terms in English and are unlikely to need explanation. Less common terms are easy to find online if the reader wishes.

And then there's food. The Russian text of *My Dreadful Body* footnotes some dishes but not others. Some names are written in Azeri; others are not. In some cases, such as *kutaby*, we've added stealth glosses to describe the dishes in brief. *Kutaby*, by the way, is a transliteration from the Russian transliteration of the Azeri *qutabı*. Another dish, *plov*, is often translated as "pilaf," though we elected to add a phrase mentioning rice. Plov also has a high profile online and the word is the same in Russian and Azeri, among other languages. We left *lobio*, the Georgian name for numerous delicious bean dishes, alone, too; Russian and Azeri both borrow it.

Finally, both for this note and for the novella itself, there is verse. The eleventh chapter, "Belly" concludes with what Djabbarova's footnote calls a traditional Azerbaijani lullaby. She presents small chunks of the lullaby in Azeri, alternating them with Russian translations and her own responses or commentary, which are indented in the text. Those alternated lines are followed by several more stanzas of italicized verse that revisit many of the topics in the novella. Those final lines of verse are a fitting end to *My Dreadful Body*, both as a summary and a new formal element in Djabbarova's text. After eleven chapters, Djabbarova's unique combination of languages and literary devices adds a new element to her careful kaleidoscope of words and themes.

Contrary to stereotype, translation is not a lonely job. I always have my authors' voices in my head when I work on their books, whether I'm at my desk or not. That means I'm especially grateful for all the help that Egana Djabbarova patiently provided when I was finishing my final draft of the translation. She answered many questions for me since lots of Russian and English words have so many meanings that it can be difficult to first pinpoint an author's intent and then identify a fitting English translation. Given that Djabbarova also writes poetry, I wasn't sure, for example, if one word referred to a sink (the kind in a bathroom) or a shell (the kind that covers a snail). It would have been a stretch for that particular passage to invoke a metaphorical shell, but I wanted to be sure. Stranger things have happened. (It's a sink.) And then there was the troublesome Russian word that means both "stairs" and "ladder." (It's stairs.) English sometimes creates odd ambiguities, too, and I occasionally needed to change a word or two, with the author's permission, in order to avoid misunderstandings. In one sentence, we transformed a colon to a semicolon to be sure there wouldn't be confusion when punctuation marks are mentioned metaphorically. Djabbarova's warmth and trust mean as much to me as her technical help—translation is a very intimate process that brings me deep into my authors' minds.

Finally, my heartfelt thanks to everyone who reads this English translation of *My Dreadful Body*. This novella has come to mean more to me than I had ever expected, thanks to Djabbarova's unique combination of writing and insight. I hope that my translation conveys the many ways I appreciate *My Dreadful Body* so that you, its readers, may come to appreciate it, too.

Lisa C. Hayden

For more:

"OUTSIDE: Russian Poets Abroad Speak: A Reading by Egana Dzhabbarova" (Amherst Center for Russian Culture, May 2, 2025) is a wonderful chance to hear Djabbarova read some of her poetry and speak about her life and languages. The event was organized and hosted by Polina Barskova (UC Berkeley) and Catherine Ciepiela (Amherst College).

https://www.amherst.edu/academiclife/departments/russian/acrc/events/outside-russian-poets-abroad-speak-a-reading-by-egana-dzhabbarova

"New Nation, New Alphabet: Azerbaijani Children's Books in the 1990's" (Cotsen Children's Library blog) offers an excellent and relatively simple introduction to alphabets used in Azerbaijan.

https://blogs.princeton.edu/cotsen/tag/azerbaijani-alphabet

EGANA DJABBAROVA, born in 1992 into an Azerbaijani family in Yekaterinburg, Russia, is a poet, essayist, and scholar. She is the author of several collections of poetry. Having been forced to flee Russia in 2024, she lives in Hamburg, Germany.

LISA C. HAYDEN is a literary translator who received her MA in Russian literature from the University of Pennsylvania. She spent six years in Moscow and lives in Maine.

***OBLIVION*
BY SERGEI LEBEDEV**

In one of the first 21st century Russian novels to probe the legacy of the Soviet prison camp system, a young man travels to the vast wastelands of the Far North to uncover the truth about a shadowy neighbor who saved his life, and whom he knows only as Grandfather II. Emerging from today's Russia, where the ills of the past are being forcefully erased from public memory, this masterful novel represents an epic literary attempt to rescue history from the brink of oblivion.

***THE YEAR OF THE COMET*
BY SERGEI LEBEDEV**

A story of a Russian boyhood and coming of age as the Soviet Union is on the brink of collapse. Lebedev depicts a vast empire coming apart at the seams, transforming a very public moment into something tender and personal, and writes with stunning beauty and shattering insight about childhood and the growing consciousness of a boy in the world.

***UNTRACEABLE*
BY SERGEI LEBEDEV**

An extraordinary Russian novel about poisons of all kinds: physical, moral and political. Professor Kalitin is a ruthless, narcissistic chemist who has developed an untraceable lethal poison called Neophyte while working in a secret city on an island in the Russian far east. When the Soviet Union collapses, he defects to the West in a riveting tale through which Lebedev probes the ethical responsibilities of scientists providing modern tyrants with ever newer instruments of retribution and control.

A PRESENT PAST
BY SERGEI LEBEDEV

The Soviet and post-Soviet world, with its untold multitude of crimes, is a natural breeding ground for ghost stories. No one writes them more movingly than Russian author Sergei Lebedev, who in this stunning volume probes a collective guilty conscience marked by otherworldliness and the denial of misdeeds. These eleven tales share a mystical topography in which the legacy of totalitarian regimes is ever-present.

THE BISHOP'S BEDROOM
BY PIERO CHIARA

World War Two has just come to an end and there's a yearning for renewal. A man in his thirties is sailing on Lake Maggiore in northern Italy, hoping to put off the inevitable return to work. Dropping anchor in a small, fashionable port, he meets the enigmatic owner of a nearby villa. The two form an uneasy bond, recognizing in each other a shared taste for idling and erotic adventure. A sultry, stylish psychological thriller executed with supreme literary finesse.

UGLINESS
BY MOSHTARI HILAL

How do power and beauty join forces to determine who is considered ugly? What role does that ugliness play in fomenting hatred? Moshtari Hilal, an Afghan-born author and artist, has written a touching, intimate, and highly political book. With a profound mix of essay, poetry, her own drawings, and cultural and social history of the body, Hilal asks: Why are we afraid of ugliness?

THE EYE
BY PHILIPPE COSTAMAGNA

It's a rare and secret profession, comprising a few dozen people around the world equipped with a mysterious mixture of knowledge and innate sensibility. Summoned to Swiss bank vaults, Fifth Avenue apartments, and Tokyo storerooms, they are entrusted by collectors, dealers, and museums to decide if a coveted picture is real or fake and to determine if it was painted by Leonardo da Vinci or Raphael. *The Eye* lifts the veil on the rarified world of connoisseurs devoted to the authentication and discovery of Old Master artworks.

THE ANIMAL GAZER
BY EDGARDO FRANZOSINI

A hypnotic novel inspired by the strange and fascinating life of sculptor Rembrandt Bugatti, brother of the fabled automaker. Bugatti obsessively observes and sculpts the baboons, giraffes, and panthers in European zoos, finding empathy with their plight and identifying with their life in captivity. Rembrandt Bugatti's work, now being rediscovered, is displayed in major art museums around the world and routinely fetches large sums at auction. Edgardo Franzosini recreates the young artist's life with intense lyricism, passion, and sensitivity.

ALLMEN AND THE DRAGONFLIES
BY MARTIN SUTER

Johann Friedrich von Allmen has exhausted his family fortune by living in Old World grandeur despite present-day financial constraints. Forced to downscale, Allmen inhabits the garden house of his former Zurich estate, attended by his Guatemalan butler, Carlos. This is the first of a series of humorous, fast-paced detective novels devoted to a memorable gentleman thief. A thrilling art heist escapade infused with European high culture and luxury that doesn't shy away from the darker side of human nature.

THE MADELEINE PROJECT
by Clara Beaudoux

A young woman moves into a Paris apartment and discovers a storage room filled with the belongings of the previous owner, a certain Madeleine who died in her late nineties, and whose treasured possessions nobody seems to want. In an audacious act of journalism driven by personal curiosity and humane tenderness, Clara Beaudoux embarks on *The Madeleine Project*, documenting what she finds on Twitter with text and photographs, introducing the world to an unsung 20th century figure.

ADUA
by Igiaba Scego

Adua, an immigrant from Somalia to Italy, has lived in Rome for nearly forty years. She came seeking freedom from a strict father and an oppressive regime, but her dreams of film stardom ended in shame. Now that the civil war in Somalia is over, her homeland calls her. She must decide whether to return and reclaim her inheritance, but also how to take charge of her own story and build a future.

THE 6:41 TO PARIS
by Jean-Philippe Blondel

Cécile, a stylish 47-year-old, has spent the weekend visiting her parents outside Paris. By Monday morning, she's exhausted. These trips back home are stressful and she settles into a train compartment with an empty seat beside her. But it's soon occupied by a man she recognizes as Philippe Leduc, with whom she had a passionate affair that ended in her brutal humiliation 30 years ago. In the fraught hour and a half that ensues, Cécile and Philippe hurtle towards the French capital in a psychological thriller about the pain and promise of past romance.

THE MADONNA OF NOTRE DAME
by Alexis Ragougneau

Fifty thousand people jam into Notre Dame Cathedral to celebrate the Feast of the Assumption. The next morning, a beautiful young woman clothed in white kneels at prayer in a cathedral side chapel. But when someone accidentally bumps against her, her body collapses. She has been murdered. This thrilling novel illuminates shadowy corners of the world's most famous cathedral, shedding light on good and evil with suspense, compassion and wry humor.

THE LAST WEYNFELDT
by Martin Suter

Adrian Weynfeldt is an art expert in an international auction house, a bachelor in his mid-fifties living in a grand Zurich apartment filled with costly paintings and antiques. Always correct and well-mannered, he's given up on love until one night—entirely out of character for him—Weynfeldt decides to take home a ravishing but unaccountable young woman and gets embroiled in an art forgery scheme that threatens his buttoned up existence. This refined page-turner moves behind elegant bourgeois facades into darker recesses of the heart.

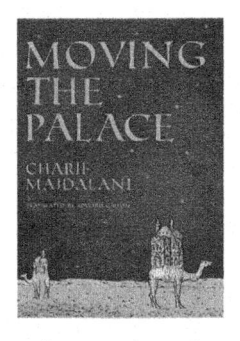

MOVING THE PALACE
by Charif Majdalani

A young Lebanese adventurer explores the wilds of Africa, encountering an eccentric English colonel in Sudan and enlisting in his service. In this lush chronicle of far-flung adventure, the military recruit crosses paths with a compatriot who has dismantled a sumptuous palace and is transporting it across the continent on a camel caravan. This is a captivating modern-day Odyssey in the tradition of Bruce Chatwin and Paul Theroux.

New Vessel Press

To purchase these titles and for more information please visit newvesselpress.com.